I0542409

ExStream Love

DO IT AGAIN

KATHRYN LIVELY

Do It Again
ISBN # 978-1-78686-382-9
©Copyright Kathryn Lively 2018
Cover Art by Erin Dameron-Hill ©Copyright December 2018
Interior text design by Claire Siemaszkiewicz
Totally Bound Publishing

Published in 2018 by Totally Bound Publishing, United Kingdom.

DO IT AGAIN

Dedication

The day I received my first AM/FM radio and found the pop/rock station changed my life. Music inspires me to write and I wish to thank all the amazing ladies who have seen me through the light and dark: Joan J., Lita, Carole, Janis, Cyndi, Pat, Ann and Nancy, Kate and Cindy, Tina, Janet, Aretha, Stevie, Christine, Joan B., Joni, Beyoncé, Alanis, Gloria, Madonna, Debbie H., Siouxsie, Linda R., Sinead, Karen, Carly, Cher, Sister Rosetta, Grace J., Grace S., Gaga…and everybody in between.

Also, part of the first chapter was inspired by memories of a Tom Petty concert I attended in 1989. The Full Moon Fever tour remains one of the best live shows I've ever seen.
R.I.P., Tom.

Chapter One

"Come see, come see. Remember meeeeee…"

Whoa. Who here is singing one of my favorite songs? A classic one at that, not a pop-radio pleaser from his latest LP. She doubted the majority of girls in this crowd could name a Bowie tune pre-*Let's Dance*, they all looked so nubile.

Her as well, but she'd been raised on the classics.

Randi Marsh looked away from the giant, dirty mirror spanning the sinks. She regretted the move seconds later when an elbow nudged her right side. She'd managed to claim this prime position in the closest bathroom to the coliseum floor when she arrived. She, along with the gaggle of young women crowding the mirror, had about five minutes to primp before the doors opened to admit concertgoers to the general seating area. Somebody must have interpreted her momentary lapse of focus as intent to leave her coveted spot.

Why am I even doing this? she asked herself as a clump of mascara stung the corner of her right eye. She never wore makeup, not to school or even when her parents dragged her to church or work socials. She'd have deigned to come see a white-hot rock band live with a bare face, if not for a momentary urge to compete with the clique of rich snobs from school, bragging about their plans to get noticed and get backstage. Like they had a shot, either—this show had been sold out for weeks. Thousands of young women preened and pouted around the venue, and tonight they'd vie for the band's attention. *What are the odds of being singled out by a rock star?*

Randi was a good girl, too. If a roadie plucked her from the crowd, the men of Black Alchemy would be disappointed when she asked to see their equipment—meaning their guitars, not their dicks.

The sugary mist expelled from a dozen or so aerosol cans hung in the air and Randi fought the urge to sneeze. She checked her reflection once more—one in a sea of tarted-up, smoldering glances swathed in bright blue eye shadows and pink blushes—and backed toward the paper towel dispensers. Whoever sang that short line from one of her favorite songs now hummed the rest of the refrain, and it attracted Randi like a siren's call.

On the rock music scale, Black Alchemy rested as far as possible from Bowie. Hell, much as she liked them, they didn't even exist on the same plane. All of the British singer's personas—Ziggy, Halloween Jack, the Thin White Duke—evoked a strange sensuality and commanded listeners to think about the songs. Black Alchemy's music projected a twenty-hour party soaked in whiskey and bodily fluids. Their lyrics were simplistic, and Randi suspected they'd never win awards for them, but she loved their guitar solos.

She loved most styles of music, despite her criticisms, and took any opportunity to see a live show. The tall brunette in the torn jeans and ponytail to her waist, next to her at the dispensers, stood to tempt her away from the opening chords.

Damn, we're twins. Well, not as such. Randi had teased her blonde hair into spikes and shards, and a tight black miniskirt — smuggled in her purse out of parental view and donned in the car after she parked — limited her stride. She saw their common link in the T-shirts they wore. Randi sported her first concert souvenir, a black raglan from a band her father had taken her to see three years prior. The woman drying her hands represented a much earlier show from the same group.

Randi grabbed a brown paper towel and folded it into a triangle. "Love your shirt," she said with a nod and dabbed at her tearing eye with the limp corner.

The young woman had about a foot's height on her. She smiled and her gaze panned down her chest to the band logo. "Likewise." She sounded older, maybe twenties or better. A good few years more than Randi's seventeen. "That tour was awesome, too. I saw 'em ten times that year."

"Wow." Randi cringed at her spontaneous awe, thinking she came off like a child. She'd attended just one concert from the tour with her father, but she wasn't about to admit that here. "I'm guessing this isn't your first time seeing Black Alchemy, huh?"

The woman gave a shrug, her lip quirking to one side. "First time so far, but I'm actually here for the opener." She stuck out her hand. "I'm Kristy."

"Randi. I heard your singing. What other bands are you into?"

She must have said the magic word. Kristy's eyes sparkled and her face softened into a dreamlike state. Words streamed from pink lips shining with gloss and carried Randi from the crowded ladies room into the din of the corridor lining the circular venue. They strolled past T-shirt vendors and concession stands tempting passersby with the aroma of fresh-popped corn, but they kept walking and talking music.

As she listened to the other woman wax on, Randi pegged Kristy as older than she'd suspected — maybe early thirties. She'd seen everybody, so she claimed in a rambling roll call of rock in vast arenas and piss-stained nightclubs. Randi sensed her skin darkening to a green tint as she absorbed it. It had taken weeks of wheedling and vows to hit the books to get permission to be here tonight.

"How do you afford it all?" she asked as they neared the entrance to the floor.

Kristy laughed. "Priorities. I do what I love, and I love live music. That's where I invest my money."

Randi thought of the joint bank account her parents wouldn't let her touch. She'd be happy with a new guitar. A few hundred bucks, no biggie, but her mother argued she needed every cent for college. *Bleh.* Kristy talked as though she forewent food and clean underwear just to hear Steven Tyler croon *Sweet Emotion* while sweating under klieg lights.

Yeah, she could give up a few luxuries. Makeup, no problem.

"Do you play?" Randi asked.

Kristy shook her head. "I sing, though. I think I'm pretty good, but you know how the business is. Singers are a dime a dozen. It takes somebody with a special something to make it."

"I hear you."

The second she crossed the threshold with her new friend she broke her promise to Mom and Dad to watch the show from a seat in the upper decks. No chairs set up on the ground implied festival seating for the stage area, an arrangement made dangerous years ago during a concert in Cincinnati where several people had perished during a stampede. A slight chill settled over Randi's skin with every step deeper into the crowd gathered on the concrete surface. Some sat, while others hovered while shifting their feet. Kristy continued to chat with her and inch closer to the stage.

"I met Zane a few years ago when they were an opener," she explained, referring to the frontman of Snake Pit, the opening act. "They're going to try out a few new songs tonight."

"Cool." Randi cared little, if at all, for their current hit. The lyrics bordered on misogyny and the guitar work sounded sloppy. Had she not wanted a good spot for Black Alchemy she'd have come late and missed out on the group.

"Zane's going to wear his *Hee Haw* coveralls," Kristy snickered.

Hell of a fashion statement, Randi decided. She itched to ask if Kristy was a groupie but feared a hostile reaction. Her dearth of sexual knowledge aside, she knew some mechanics and that groupies often put out in order to receive benefits—backstage access, maybe autographs and swag.

The clap.

Her mother's voice echoed in her brain, admonishing her. *'You come right home afterward. Don't be like those girls who flash their goods.'*

She looked down at her Rush shirt, which was nearly flat. *Who'd notice if I did?*

Snake Pit had a modest setup, what Randi perceived as the bare minimum in lighting and equipment. Three microphone stands equidistant from each other toward the front, and two Fenders rested on stands stage right. Randi, wanting a closer look, edged toward that side but paused behind a group of people clustered together.

"If you want to move up, go ahead," Kristy encouraged her. "I'm heading that way myself."

"Oh, I don't know if I want to be —"

Randi lost the opportunity to finish the thought. A long-haired roadie had stepped up to the middle microphone and uttered a deep-voiced, "Check," that echoed through the venue. Everybody on the floor took this as a sign to expect Snake Pit to come charging out to begin the show, and bodies panicked and surged. People behind Randi pushed forward and she squealed, her mother shaming her in her head. *'How can I face my bridge club, telling them you died at a Snake Pit concert?'*

Rather than wait to become roadkill, Randi moved with the crowd and in seconds she was pressed up against the stage, a laughing Kristy at her side. "You think they're all eager to get this started?" the older woman called, having to shout over the din of restless rock fans so Randi could hear. Randi's heartbeat pounded in her ears, overpowering other noises surrounding her. The jolt of adrenaline from the lightning-fast sprint to the lip kept her attention focused to the front. She patted her thigh, feeling for the rectangular indent in her skirt pocket. Good, she still had her license and the car key. Assuming she survived the crush of fans, her parents wouldn't be happy to discover she'd been stranded.

"I am, at least," she hollered back. At this point, though, she wanted Snake Pit on and off in hopes the crowd relaxed some in between acts. When the five musicians comprising the first band strutted out to the strains of a steady drum beat, Randi winced from the pain searing through her skull. Too close, too loud, too much body odor. Every breath became a struggle as raised arms invaded her personal space. Her chest flattened against the stage and her neck kinked and turned sore as she had to look up to see the action.

They were eye level with thick-heeled boots—leopard prints and black laces to complement leather pants and vests, no shirts. Snake Pit's lead guitarist, wailing on a yellow Stratocaster with painted-on flames licking up past the whammy bar, just missed her fingers as he danced close to the edge to tease the crowd. Randi glanced upward for an eyeful of chest and underarm hair and pale, bare arms glistening with sweat.

He caught her eye and stuck out his tongue, flicking it in some kind of lurid 'come hither' signal. *Not on your life, bud.* Randi shifted her attention toward the drums.

Snake Pit raged through their set, each song more rambling and explicit than the last. Randi, having never heard anything beyond their one radio hit, prayed her thanks to every deity that her parents hadn't made good on an earlier threat to chaperone her. As much as she loved music, Snake Pit had a ways to go before achieving something similar to it. This was noise, and now that she was almost deaf she wondered if she'd get to enjoy Black Alchemy at all.

The lead singer, his black hair teased into an explosion around his gaunt face, pumped a fist in the air as their final number crashed to a close. "Fuck you very much, San Bernardino! We are Snake Pit!" he hollered to a rash of cheering. "Get your bloody asses ready for Black Alchemy."

He looked down, a sparkle in his kohl-rimmed eyes and a comic book villain's grin showing off crooked teeth. Randi met his gaze for a split second — enough to spark his interest. With Kristy nearby, though, she figured the musician had spotted a familiar face. But as the rest of the band trudged away he towered over a cluster of people, their arms waving like seagrass, fingers wriggling for even the slightest touch of celebrity.

Randi kept to herself, hands pinned to her front to protect the contents of her skirt pocket.

"Zane! Over here!" Kristy called, and Zane dipped down and extended both arms.

One for Kristy, one for her.

What? Okay, so the guy wanted to gift a 'fan' with casual physical contact. She'd seen videos where musicians grazed fingertips with zealous crowds. Randi could think of a dozen rock stars she'd prefer to greet — hell, more than that — but figured the chance to be a greater part of a concert didn't happen every day.

He wasn't a teen mag cover-model type, but Zane was cute, in a heroin chic kind of way.

She reached up to shake his hand, at the same time he tugged Kristy up onstage. That was when Randi saw the bassist and rhythm guitarist lurking behind him. They hadn't taken off as she first thought.

They were grabbing her arm and encouraging the people around her to hoist her high.

"Hey!" she cried. One pair of arms — it was hard to tell for all the movement — tightened around her waist and she kicked upward as her captor whirled her in a circle. Kristy and Zane skedaddled ahead of her and disappeared into the wings. Which one of these snakes had her? "Put me down. I can walk, you know."

"Soon, love," sounded a voice like smoke in her ear. "You're a feisty one, eh?"

Randi struggled in his grip and whooped when the bassist — she discovered as such when the guitarist stepped for a moment into her line of vision — twirled her like she was weightless and settled her body over his shoulder. She looked out into venue at the sea of shadowed faces and limbs — thousands of people roaring approval for a rock star's conquest. She squinted in vain to find anyone from school, no doubt cursing Randi's so-called good fortune.

Please, none of y'all tell my parents this is happening.

Drummer Greg Orville plodded offstage first, as usual, without giving Derek Hynde a second glance. The band's young manager was used to the performer's aloof behavior, and wouldn't begrudge Greg his desire for peace. As Snake Pit's elder statesman, Greg eschewed the sex and drugs components of the lifestyle and darted straight for his motorcycle after each show. By the time the rest of group exited to let the roadies change sets he'd be in his hotel room with a thick book and an eighty-proof nightcap.

Both sounded terrific to Derek right about now. *Anywhere but here.*

One by one the rest of the band came backstage, dressed like pornographic wasps and toting souvenirs of the female variety. *Fuckin' fantastic.* He recognized the one with Zane — Kelly, Kasey, something close to that — and offered a partial smile when she waggled her fingers at him in a cutesy wave.

"We'll be taking a break before the hotel, right?" Zane Porter called to him.

"Wear a condom this time, would you?" Derek shot back. He got the finger from the girl in response. *Hey, it's cheaper than a child support suit.* He cringed, thinking back to a rather large check dashed off to some redhead bouncing a newborn on her hip, a boy with the bassist's nose and blue eyes. It covered an agreement to refrain from pursuing further payments but didn't keep her lips zipped when the tabloids came sniffing.

Speak of the horny devil…

Hal Kaiser passed by with a shit-eating grin and an arm wrapped around a pair of shapely legs, one heel hanging by the woman's arched foot. Over Hal's shoulder, his captive pounded on his back and demanded her freedom.

She caught Derek's stare as Hal kept walking. "Oh, don't mind me. No need to assist. I got this under control," she drawled, then hung limp in defeat.

"Fair enough," Derek muttered. Any other time, he'd have let the band enjoy their 'booty', so to speak. This bird, however, didn't express the hard-to-get attitude other groupies had. Some liked to bite and scratch, leaving Derek to presume their aggressive behavior was designed to turn on the musicians they targeted.

This girl—and she was a girl, no doubt, teetering on the edge of legal-age—seemed to want to be somewhere else, instead of being carried into the dressing room.

Derek started toward the door about to close Snake Pit off from the rest of the world when the loudest expletive he'd heard today sounded from the truck bay. *Greg.* He needed to check on that before the drummer punched an innocent bystander.

He grabbed the nearest red shirt, a venue employee charged with helping out the crew. "Keep an eye on them, and if the blonde looks like she needs assistance, give it," he ordered before stomping out into the dry California heat.

He wanted to walk far away, through the tall chain link fences cordoning off the buses and equipment trucks and up the highway. Whichever direction took him to the nearest airport and back to London, he was all for it. He hated this job—he was nothing more than a glorified babysitter for a quintet of spoiled musicians. Greg aside, they lacked talent and drive, yet their label hemorrhaged money to promote their sophomore album and American breakthrough. *'Don't worry, just let them be,'* his father—and boss—had advised at the start of the tour. Snake Pit were green for the most part, yes, but after a few weeks they'd let off their steam and settle into a routine of responsible behavior.

So Derek had been told. He was still waiting.

Three months after Da's speech, most of the band had all but become walking STDs. What he wouldn't give for the opportunity to scout a group to mold from the ground up, a discovery to influence and encourage. He wanted to walk into a bar one night and be blown away by an unsigned band, much like the time Brian Epstein had spotted a charming quartet at a club in Liverpool. The Snake Pit job was a hand-me-down, given to him because nobody else in Da's organization wanted it.

Paying my dues, my arse.

He found Greg pacing alongside his motorcycle, borrowed from a stateside friend for the duration of the North American leg. Derek had envied the drummer's decision to ride the tour route on his own and skip the daily melee of weed and porn and spunk coating the bus seats. The budget hadn't allowed Derek such peace, and he cursed his own thrifty tendencies. He was saving for a house, and he forced himself to believe it was worth the headaches Snake Pit gave him.

"Fuck me. Bugger all." The language, salty as the air, softened in volume as Derek reached the scene. Greg pulled a wrinkled cigarette pack from his vest pocket and patted his skin-tight pants for a lighter. As Derek saw no visible, cigarette lighter-shaped indentations, he offered his own and coughed at the first expulsion of smoke. He looked down to where Greg was pointing to the lighted end at the flat front tire.

"I hate American highways," the drummer groused. "Bloody near got flattened by a van on the ride here, and now I'm stuck in this hole."

"Maybe it's not so bad. You haven't had much maintenance done on this thing, and I doubt Mick was responsible enough to—" As Derek spoke, he bent to inspect the damage and quieted on finding the culprit. He reached to tug on the nail, but Greg kneed him away.

"Leave it. I don't want it wrecked any further." The man's anger cut through his voice. "Get somebody here to repair it, and the sooner the better."

"What, this late?" Derek let the activity around them distract him. He'd never been to the California coast before—until this point, he'd kept to overseeing regional tours back home while more seasoned managers in Da's firm handled the bigger acts. Where would he find a mechanic after hours with a replacement tire for a foreign motorcycle? Granted, they were close to Los Angeles, but Derek doubted he'd have assistance over in due time to satisfy Greg.

Greg was the sane one in the band but looked close to losing it. Derek couldn't afford to have him unhappy. The man had threatened more than once on this tour to breach his contract and walk.

"You're the bloody manager, Derek. Manage it," Greg barked, and took a long drag on his cigarette.

"Fine. I'll see what I can do, but I don't know how long before somebody gets here. Even then, they might want to tow this thing to some garage." A mechanic realizing he'd be dealing with rock stars was sure to see big money in his future, too, and perhaps take his time. At least they had a few days in the area for shows, but with Greg grounded it meant one unpleasant fact.

"As long as it's fixed so I don't have to get on the bus," Greg said as he stormed off to a less populated area, where Derek suspected he'd brood.

Well, bugger.

He heard the first notes of the headliner's opening number, followed by an explosion of fan gratitude. The venue had a first aid station behind the stage, and Derek remembered seeing a phone there. He considered alternative options for Greg on the short walk over — he could arrange for a taxi, or else convince the drummer to ride back in the headliner's bus. Both bands were staying in the same hotel this time, and Wayne and Ginge were a smidge more subdued compared to their opening act.

A few fans lay on cots for treatment — hydration, an EMT explained — so Derek searched the yellow pages next to the phone and found a winner on the first try. The mechanic also dealt in Italian and German models and would replace the tire on site, for cash.

Everything Derek had in his wallet. *Bugger.* He'd pay it if it meant preventing discord among the Snake Pit lineup. For certain, the rest of the band wouldn't want Greg on the bus, spoiling their good time. Derek started back to the bay, patting his back pants pocket as he thought of how he might talk the mechanic into taking the travelers' checks instead.

He saw no sign of the drummer near the motorcycle, nor was Greg lurking close enough to watch the opener. He'd either gone to the loo or had skulked deeper into isolation. No sense checking the bus, which was still parked close to the exit.

With a sigh and a shake of his head, he turned toward the party raging in the makeshift green room. Greg might not be partaking of the merriment, but maybe somebody had caught sight of him going somewhere.

He heard music, a ripping good guitar solo. *Highway Star*, one of his favorites. Who was playing, though? Neither guitarist in Snake Pit had the chops for that advanced a number. They performed like the punk bands of the Seventies, with minimal chords and rapid-sung lyrics.

Derek opened the door and let out the sound, richer and fuller than anything he'd expected from the band since beginning the tour. He expected to find he'd been mistaken about the live guitar, that somebody had brought in a tape player while everybody paired off with a bird. The last thing he thought to see tonight was the young woman Hal had carried off caveman-like, showing him up on his own guitar.

Bloody hell. The girl can play. Now if only…

As the thought formed, she acted on his wishes. She sang, her voice bold and rich, full of melody and star quality.

He smiled, basking in his Brian Epstein moment.

* * * *

Randi refused everything offered to her, from the mystery drink in the red plastic cup to the cocaine scraped into neat, thin lines atop a used Spanish textbook somebody had found in the room. The venue hadn't afforded Snake Pit fancy digs for their after-show soiree, but Randi noticed the musicians appeared too inebriated to care. Or else, they'd come off such a mighty high from their set that they were willing to party in a pigsty if directed to one.

At least Hal—she'd learned his name after Kristy squealed at him—had let her go. When she showed no signs of giving in to his sloppy attempts at seduction, he grunted and drifted to the other side of the room to flirt with a pair of groupies who entered the green room on their own. Both wore heavy makeup and short shorts to match their bedazzled tank tops. One had her backstage pass affixed to the visible lower curve of her butt.

Classy.

Randi was miserable, alone in a room full of people and wanting to return to the concert. Twice she'd tried to excuse herself but either Kristy or Zane would push her back to the couch and implore her to hang around. "Party's just getting started, love." Zane had that on repeat on his tongue. Randi felt like a hostage—she wanted to see Black Alchemy. She wasn't getting her ticket money's worth here.

"More like an orgy," Randi muttered, but Zane didn't hear for Kristy's mouth sucking on one side of his face. Disgusted, Randi turned away and studied the long tables along one wall, loaded with snacks and sweets. Her stomach rumbled, but she refused to touch anything here. The brownies could have pot in them, or LSD in the punch. She'd leave this place sober with her virtue intact, the sooner the better.

"What'd you birds think of the show?" Zane was asking, his head turning between them. "We rocked it tonight, eh?"

"Damn right you did, hon." Kristy snuggled into Zane's side, having devolved into a giggling groupie since coming backstage. Randi found it difficult to believe this was the same young woman with whom she'd had an intelligent conversation about music before the concert began.

The praise appeared to bolster the singer. He puffed up and smiled, then waited for Randi's response. The background noise lowered in volume, as though the crowd were giving their attention to the moment. Randi shrugged. "You guys were all right, I guess."

"Wot?"

Wrong answer.

Zane's brows scrunched and he pushed his lips into a snarl. "So you're a critic, then? What's a girl like you know about good music?"

"Enough to recognize it when I hear it. I'm still waiting."

A collective *ooooh* rippled through the room, as though challenging Zane to get Randi to eat her words. The eyes on her intimidated her, and Kristy's laughing off the remark didn't defuse the situation. Randi's heart beat fast, but she figured maybe the insult was enough to get her ejected from the green room so she could rejoin the concert.

Rather than oust her, Zane snapped his fingers toward the guitarist who'd snickered at her when Hal the bassist had abducted her. Ian, as he was called, came forward with his guitar and motioned for somebody to plug in the small practice amp by the sofa.

"Right, follow my lead," Zane ordered and counted off the lead-in for Ian to play. The singer then let forth some improvised lyrics of the 'oh baby-love to love you' variety while Ian matched with the music.

Yeah, girl, gonna shag you all through the night
Gonna give you great delight
Love you, baby, all night long

It's why I'm singing you this song

On it went, with his gaze pinned to her the entire time. Randi wanted to shrink under the sofa cushion.

After another minute Zane made a chopping motion with his hand and the impromptu recital ended to the small crowd's applause. He regarded Randi with a smirk. "Came up with that from the top of my head."

It showed. Randi stood and took the warm, tobacco-scented air into her lungs. She was done hating how her night had turned out, and whenever she felt down she turned to the one thing guaranteed to revive her spirits.

She held out her hand to Ian and nodded to the Strat. The guitarist paused, then erupted in snorting laughter.

"Go on, then," Zane egged on his bandmate. "Let her have a go at it. Be nice to be entertained by 'Polly Wolly Doodle,' or such."

Laughter. Jokes. Derision. Randi was used to it, having spent many a group lesson as the sole female. Girls were supposed to perform classical numbers or hippie-folk ballads on acoustic instruments and leave the heavy lifting to people with balls.

Well, she had them as well. Unlike Ian, she knew more than a few chords.

He stepped aside while she adjusted the strap and tested the weight of the Strat in her grip. Ian handed her a pick and she sensed a current rush through her, like grasping a talisman for energy and luck. Without thinking too hard, she let a force guide the fingers of her left hand over the fret and she launched into one of her dad's favorites, *Highway Star*. Memories rushed to the forefront of her consciousness, and she closed her eyes to seal off the crowd and concentrate on what made her most happy.

Her father played guitar, and piano and violin. He never worked at the professional level—it was a hobby he enjoyed and he mimicked the best. Call out a tune big on the radio, and he'd play and sing with near accuracy. When ten-year-old Randi had asked to learn, he'd taught her songs from his favorite rock album.

She opened her eyes when she realized in the moment she was singing along to the music, something she didn't always do. All around, people stared agog. Zane looked embarrassed to sit there, and Kristy was no longer pawing him. Everybody regarded her with stone silence, unmoving and enrapt.

It damn near frightened her, and she ended on an abrupt note without finishing.

"I-I have to go," she said, and tore the Strat from her body. She handed it to Ian before turning on her heel to dash for the door.

A man blocked her path. "Where are you going, love?"

"Out. Away from here." A creeping urgency came over Randi. Never mind heading back to catch the remainder of the Black Alchemy set. She wanted to go home and play her own guitar, find her comfort in the privacy of her room. Perform for her stuffed animals and the dog.

This man's clothes set him apart from the rest of the group. He wore a suit and had a neat trim and straight teeth. He looked professional, in charge, and seemed the type to expel unauthorized teen girls from backstage. She wouldn't wait for that to happen.

"Let me through," she whined.

Behind her, voices whispered in disbelief. "How the hell does she play like that? That song's ten years old. She's got to be too young to know it!"

"I'll walk you out, at least." He put his hand on her arm, giving her no other option but to concede. As they left, a body came close to her back, as though rushing her into the open. It made her leery and she turned around, seeing that it was Snake Pit's drummer.

"Fancy finding you inside," her escort said to him.

"Have to kill time somewhere before my ride gets fixed." The musician pointed a lit cigarette at her. "If you don't sign her on the spot, Derek, you're a bloody fool."

"I'll handle it, Greg. Off you pop."

Greg nodded at her before disappearing. "You ever need a drummer, you got one."

"I don't need a drummer. I need a payphone," she called to his retreating back. Turning to Derek, who still clutched her arm, she jerked in an attempt to free herself. "I'll scream," she threatened.

"I wish you wouldn't. You'll ruin that lovely voice."

"You can let go. I won't run away. Not in these damn shoes."

"What's your name, love?"

"What's it matter?" Randi asked. "Soon as I get out of here I'm going home and you're off to the next stop on the tour. I'm assuming you're with the band." She nodded to where Greg had walked away.

Derek gave her a smile, soft and natural, and loosened his touch but didn't yet pull away. His kept his hand close to her arm, as though trying to soak up some radiant talent. "You're quite good with the guitar."

"Thanks." She rubbed the spot where Derek had grasped her and took a step back. What was stopping her from sidling further away and leaving the backstage area? Randi noticed a uniformed officer hovering by the gated partition separating the concert crowd. All she had to do was yell for help and she was home free.

This Derek, though… Handsome and kind-faced, and having some influence with the musicians here. He seemed to take music seriously, more so than the idiots with whom he associated, so she supposed that warranted him a few seconds of her time.

Also, that British accent. Smoother than Zane's. Posh. Like a drug to her ears. *Damn.*

"You take lessons, or have you learned by ear?"

He folded his arms now, assuming a non-intimidating stance. It worked, and she relaxed a bit. "Bit of both," she said. "My dad taught me a few songs, and I took group lessons for years. When I'm not doing homework I listen to records and pick melodies apart until I can fake it."

"Homework? So you're in school?" He frowned. "I didn't realize you were so young. I probably shouldn't be talking with you like this."

"What's the big deal?" she asked, irritated. "It's not like you're asking me out on a date." She pondered the idea of that. Derek had to be close to thirty. Tempting, but her parents would freak. Anyway, they would soon part ways for good, and he wouldn't remember her from Kristy or any other girl wandering around backstage.

"Besides," she added, feeling brave, "you don't know that I'm talking about college homework. Grad school, even."

He chuckled. "What is your name? I have to call you something besides 'love' or 'dearie'."

"Miranda Marsh. I go by Randi."

They shook hands. "Miranda Marsh, who goes by Randi, I am Derek Hynde. I co-manage Snake Pit and I'm twenty-eight years old."

"Yeah? I'm twenty-six."

He blinked twice, a quick gesture one saw in people trying to process impossible news like the existence of Bigfoot. Yeah, she could have shot for twenty-one, an age closer to hers that was still legal. Her skills with the guitar notwithstanding, Randi knew her age stood to work against her if she wanted to be taken seriously.

What the hell am I doing? Why try to impress this guy, when she had to get away?

"Good to know," Derek said after a brief pause, nodding. "I hope you stay on the straight and narrow."

"What? You want to know if I'm a lez?"

He chuckled. "Sober, love. Drug and drink free. Off anything that would bring you into the dreaded Twenty-Seven Club. You're not that far off, you know."

"Right." She got it now. Not straight as in het, but not a junkie. Although, not every rock musician who died after hitting the cursed birthday was under the influence of drugs or drink.

"Why does it matter to you?" she asked, folding her arms. Behind them, Kristy and Zane and the rest of Snake Pit filtered out into the open and strolled toward the buses.

"Because, Miranda Marsh" — Derek held out his hand in invitation — "if you'll let me manage you, I'll make you a star."

Chapter Two

"Ladies, gentlemen, friends who identify otherwise...I believe that's a wrap."

A smattering of applause and cheers rippled through soundstage at Randi's pronouncement. Where a normal day on the set of *Danse Macabre* — currently the most popular show on streaming network ExStream — ended with a collective sigh from an exhausted cast and crew, everybody tonight possessed an atypical energy. It wasn't that people didn't like working for Too True Productions or its top director, Randi herself— the employees enjoyed it to the point of fanaticism. Few minded retakes or long hours, since everybody got along so well. The top brass recognized, though, that people needed their 'me' time, too.

Thinking back on her decades-long career in show business, Randi decided her work behind the camera on this paranormal drama topped everything — and she'd encountered royalty, Beatles and presidents in the bloom of her youth. She soaked up the good feelings radiating in the studio, pleased to have another episode in the can.

"Be sure to get your beauty sleep, y'all," she called out as crew came out to strike the set, an interior they wouldn't need for the next episode. "We all want to be fresh and on alert for when Miss Thing arrives for her closeup." She cackled and slapped the arm of a passing grip, who grinned back.

Dash Gregory, the show's lead and husband of Gabby Randall, *Danse Macabre*'s creator and producer, walked up to Randi's director chair. "She has a name, Randi," he scolded.

"I know. I just feel like grousing, I guess." She kept her voice low in case Gabby or Lena, the other partner in Too True, stood within earshot. The next episode on schedule to shoot started a short arc featuring Steffi Corden, an actress with an interesting history. Not only was the woman Dash's former flame, but she'd come off the cancellation of her own show, another ExStream project. Following a humiliating display at a recent awards show, Steffi had seemed to be spiraling toward the D-list until Gabby had stepped in with the ultimate 'get out of obscurity' card—a multi-ep guest-starring role that Gabby wanted to spin off into a new series.

Gabby and Dash had history, having eloped as teenagers after a show in which they'd co-starred had ended. Her overbearing parents, after intercepting the honeymoon, had forced an annulment and it had led to years of estrangement, during which time they'd spent dating others and trying to stay relevant in the business. Through all their professional successes and failures, they'd never stopped loving each other.

Though Dash's relationship with Steffi had happened long before the couple reconnected, Gabby didn't consider the other actress a rival for her husband's affections. Randi knew this, and while she understood Steffi had the potential to behave as an actress should on set, she thought Gabby's idea was whack-nuts. She'd used that exact phrase when Gabby had brought up the plan.

She searched for her boss, not finding her among the throng of people milling in the studio. Odd, too, to see so many bodies this long after wrapping up a day. "Y'all can go home now," she called out, thinking how she looked forward to unwinding at her place with a drink and some late-night TV. The crowd, however, moved in a wave toward the exit, blocking the path to the parking lot.

Randi heard stifled giggles and whispers. She stole a glance at Dash, who mugged for her and held up his hands as if to plead innocence. *Bullshit.* Something was afoot.

Some crew were known to pull occasional pranks, more than once while the camera rolled. Randi loved a joke, but tonight she was finished. Drink, TV, bed — and the sooner the better.

She grabbed her jacket from the back of her director's chair and felt for her keys. "I'll see y'all tomorrow," she said.

"We're counting on it, but you're not done yet."

Randi recognized Gabby's voice in the distance. Several bodies clustered before her parted to reveal the producer and her business partner, Lena DeVito, pushing a table on wheels bearing a gigantic cake shaped like an electric guitar. Bright red fondant covered the body, offset nicely by the white pickguard and pickups. Lighted candles flickered in a row on the neck, interspersed by frets done in icing.

Off to one side sat a smaller, square cake — a gluten-free option, Randi guessed, for the few on staff with sensitivities — bearing the words, *Still Sexy at 60.*

The inevitable chorus of the birthday song, led by Gabby, rang loud in the studio and almost moved Randi to tears. Who was she kidding? She resisted bawling like a child for all her appreciation and lifted spirits. She'd been working so damn hard on this new season of *Danse Macabre*, to top what they'd accomplished last year, that she'd forgotten her own birthday! Of course, few in her inner circle of friends and family were still around to know the date…and maybe she hadn't forgotten. She wanted not to think about it.

Yet, Gabby remembered. Perhaps more people because of her. They had obviously planned this for a while. *Who could make a cake this awesome in one day?*

Dash guided her to the guitar's headstock as the last note crashed into cheers. She blew in one direction and managed to extinguish three of the six candles, and she waved for Gabby's help. When all were reduced to melting wax and smoke, Gabby and Lena brought out the paper plates.

"You sons of bitches," Randi muttered, earning a wave of laughter. "I was hoping this year I could slip under the radar."

"Come on, Randi," Gabby chided as she sliced into the red fondant. She pulled out a lopsided square — white cake with strawberry filling, which Randi loved. "You're always saying age ain't nothing but a number."

"When I'm hitting on a twenty-year-old, sure."

"I hope when I'm sixty I look as hot as you," Lena said.

"I hope I'm here to see it." Randi winked.

Gabby and Lena set to slicing up the cake while hands reached out to claim plates. Randi eased into the periphery of the crowd, taking in the chatter and merriment. She listened to idle talk about birthdays and parties, how this person helped her sister put together fifty goodie bags for her young niece's bash and how that guy spent his last three in Vegas. Well-wishers brought her out of her reverie to pay their respects and offer hugs, and Randi appreciated everybody's kindness.

Deep inside, though, a twinge of guilt knotted in her stomach until it formed a stone so heavy she thought she wouldn't be able to keep down the rest of her cake.

As the impromptu party roared on, and music played and some of the guest actors took to the bare bones set to dance, Randi set her empty plate on the craft table and looked for an out. It came when the assistant director tried an awkward pop and lock routine, to the crowd's encouragement, and she slipped away. Her motorcycle, with her helmet strapped to the seat, waited for her in studio's guarded lot, where she hopped on and fled. If anybody asked, she'd claim a stomachache.

At the moment, her heart hurt more.

* * * *

Gabby startled at the touch by her shoulder, but relaxed on finding her husband standing behind her. Dash bent low to whisper, "Randi snuck out."

"Maybe she had to go the bathroom."

Dash shook his head. "She had her keys in hand. I followed her out with some cake to give to Barney," he mentioned the guard on duty in the security booth, "and he said she got on her bike and took off."

Disappointment filled Gabby. For weeks she'd debated whether or not to surprise Randi with this party. Her primary director wasn't one to give thought to growing old, and Randi loved a good time. Gabby wanted to hold something special for her friend. *What prompted Randi to leave a celebration in her honor?*

Her gaze panned the soundstage. Cast and crew chatted and danced, unaware of anything amiss. Best to keep it so while she figured this out.

"Can you call for a ride, or have somebody drop you off at home?" she asked. "I'm going to her."

Dash took her half-eaten cake. "You don't even know where she is."

"I have a few ideas." With a quick kiss to silence further doubt, she grabbed her purse hanging from her director's chair and left.

After getting from Barney the direction in which Randi had gone, Gabby steered her car on the same route. She knew the way to Randi's home and turned onto the main road to get there when she passed the building that housed Too True Productions. She spotted Randi's motorcycle in the lot and slowed to pull in beside it.

Music drifted out of Randi's open office door. The woman had left the lights low, and Gabby crept up the hall with quiet steps at first. The idea of breaching Randi's privacy bothered her, but she was concerned for her friend. Randi had been one of the production company's first hires because Gabby trusted her skills and judgment. If something irked Randi — growing older, the job, anything serious or trivial — she longed to help.

She heard laughter, then a sigh. *That's a good sign.* Gabby moved close enough to peer in without revealing her presence. Randi sat at her desk, surrounded by memorabilia of an eclectic career. Over the decades Randi Marsh had reinvented herself many times—rock star, songwriter, actress, marvel behind the camera. When newcomers visited Too True and got the tour, they tended to want to stay in Randi's office all day.

Randi had her booted feet propped up on her desk and leaned back in her chair. She was leafing through a large book, smiling and shaking her head. Maybe she had a touch of nostalgia because of the day. Gabby decided it best to leave Randi to her thoughts but her friend's gravelly voice stopped her heart.

"I see you peeking."

Gabby let out a nervous laugh. "Sorry. Caught in the act." She took the opposite chair when Randi gestured to it. "You snuck out of your party. I hope you weren't offended by it. If I'd known you didn't want a big deal made, Dash and I could have just taken you out to dinner—"

"Don't apologize, girl." Randi leaned forward, boots to the ground now, and gave a playful smack to Gabby's arm. "That was nice, what y'all did. I guess it got to me. It's not just my birthday, but the first one without..."

The smiled faded and Randi looked away for a few seconds. No need to say anything more. Randi had lost her father several months ago, making this her first birthday without family, since her mother had passed more than a decade prior. Gabby could relate to being alone, in a way.

Randi recovered and held out the book. A photo album. "You know what these are called, right?" she asked, pointing to the pictures.

"Oh, jeez, let me guess." Gabby made a face as though to point out her ignorance of obsolete media. "It's what you used for selfies back in the olden days."

"Hush." Randi tapped a square in the top left corner of one page. "That's my friend Kristy. She married the lead singer of a two-hit wonder band called Snake Pit. They were kind of crap in the beginning, but they improved over time. After the group split he went on to score music for low-budget flicks. She was their groupie."

"Wow. For real? Like the whole plaster cast on the penis type?"

Randi shook her head. "If she did that, she never let on to me. She became a real PTA mom. Carpools, den mother duties, all that jazz. She doesn't keep any evidence of her wild past in the house for the grandkids to find, either."

On the next page Gabby saw a series of portraits, with each square decorated by a ribbon drawn in black marker. "Heaven's hall of fame," Randi said, her voice sad. She identified each person to Gabby, explaining their significance in her life and the untimely tragedies that had taken them. Overdose, overdose, suicide, car wreck, AIDS, cancer, overdose.

"This one hurt the most," Randi said of the one called Hal Kaiser. "He was kind of a jerk when we met, but we got to know each other and became good friends. He so wanted to get clean, but…" She shrugged, and Gabby understood. She'd grown up in Hollywood and seen friends succumb to similar fates can vices.

"I'm sorry."

"So am I," Randi said.

The page flipped to a series of shots of people Gabby did recognize. Randi's smile reappeared, relieving Gabby to know the course of evening was lightening up again. She looked at pictures of Randi's family, a few A-list rock legends and some mutual friends from *Wondermancer High*. Randi had had a recurring role on the show, playing Aunt Rowdy to Gabby's teen wizard. "I tell you, Gabby, that show saved my life. I believe it now. I mean, it didn't pay for squat and I wasn't on it as much as you, but if I hadn't taken the part, who knows where I'd be now?"

"I'd like to think you'd be on tour somewhere, or recording a new album."

Randi sputtered out a laugh. "Right. Some dinosaurs of rock has-been extravaganza, sponsored by brand-name adult diapers. No thanks." This wasn't the first time Randi had used the joke. More than once, she had kidded to people to shoot her if she ever considered going on the road to indulge fans in their nostalgia. Gabby laughed along with everybody else, but deep inside she knew her friend missed that part of her life. When Randi came here to work, she kept a guitar in hand. One couldn't miss the way the woman's fingers danced on the frets and picked out melodies.

"Randi," Gabby began.

"Don't say it." Randi held up a finger. "It's my birthday. If you're giving me a present, it can't be pity."

"Far from it. I never feel sorry for you, only jealousy," Gabby said. "I wish to look as good as you now when I'm sixty."

"So do I."

Huh?

Randi looked her in the eye and must have noticed her confusion. She nodded and glanced around, as though seeking out a hidden camera. "I have to tell you something, chick, and I don't know if it makes a difference, seeing it's gone this far without anybody catching on."

"What?" Gabby pondered her friend's cryptic words and assumed the most. She remembered Mrs. Marsh's cancer and a knot formed in her stomach. "Randi, you're not sick…?"

"No." Randi shook her head and chuckled. "I have been living a lie for the most part, though. When I first got into the music business, I may have fudged my age by a few years so I could come off as more professional."

"Is that all? This city is full of people who haven't gone by their real ages or noses in forever. How many years did you shave off?"

"Off? You think I'm seventy?"

Shit. Fix this, fix this now. "What? No," Gabby cried, covering her embarrassment with a laugh. "It's just that you don't act your…age…whatever it is. I'm going to shut up now."

Randi smirked. "I'm forty-nine, Gabby." She then frowned. "I think. The nineties were a blur, and I don't have a copy of my birth certificate anymore, but whatever. That sixtieth birthday bash you threw for me was a tad too soon, and I suppose it's my fault for saying anything."

"Randi, it doesn't matter how old you are, just that you're here and you do an awesome job for *Danse*." Gabby patted her arm. "For *Fallen Angel*, too, I hope."

Blech. Randi couldn't escape talk of Gabby's next plan, not even on her birthday. She loved working for Too True on *Danse Macabre* and would be happy to direct every episode until the tail end, but when Gabby had proposed Randi take on showrunner duties for the spinoff all the tension in the world had formed a tight ball in her chest. Randi liked to come in to work, do her job and go home. Taking charge of an entire show gave her more tasks to accomplish, more people to supervise and eventually she'd be responsible for casting and plotting out stories.

Gabby might love that part of television, but Randi had reincarnated enough times in this town. *Danse Macabre* would see her into an eventual retirement, but it sounded like *Fallen Angel* could kill her first.

"We'll see. ExStream still has to say yes." Randi knew, per Gabby's contract with the network, they got right of first refusal on Too True's future projects. Also, they loved *Danse* and the spike in subscriptions it brought, so they were sure to greenlight anything Gabby sent their way.

Gabby rose and straightened her clothes. "Steffi Corden will be coming by tomorrow to go over details. I'd like the two of you to meet if you have time."

"I'll be here. I'm surprised she agreed to this." Randi closed her photo album and shelved it, then propped her boots back on the desk. "She's going to wonder about ulterior motives, I'll bet."

"Let her." Gabby shrugged. "She fucked up at the awards, yeah, but she's a good actress. She's good for the part and she needs this chance if she wants to set things right for her career."

"You're not bothered by the fact she used to go out with Dash?"

"This is business," Gabby said, sounding stiff. "And that's history."

"Right." Randi's fingers itched to wrap around the neck of a guitar. She kept one in her office, but it meant having to stand and cross the room to get it. She'd wait for Gabby leave first to release her energy and frustration over this new development. She had nothing against Steffi Corden, but she'd be damned if that diva D-lister tried anything to sabotage Gabby's show.

A text noise pinged and Gabby checked her phone. "Dash is home now. I better go." She leaned down to kiss Randi's cheek. "You going to be okay here?"

"I'm fine, go home to your hubby. I just need to unwind and contemplate life." She smiled.

Gabby was almost out of the door when she glanced back. "I'm glad to hear you're younger than you actually are," she said. "It means we'll have you for ten more years than we first thought."

Lord willing. With her boss gone and the building empty, Randi got up and retrieved her guitar. The music sounded tinny without a speaker to amplify the tune she played, but in her mind a concert blasted at full volume bolstered by a cheering crowd. She'd assured Gabby she loved her job at *Danse Macabre*, but she'd be lying to herself if she didn't admit how much she missed performing on stage, no matter how often she joked about being too old to perform.

Recording new music seldom crossed her mind these days, and while she cringed at the idea of joining a roster of 'oldies' acts, she had to ask herself — *How bad can it be?* Maybe a show here or there in an L.A. club, just the hits to an appreciative audience. Randi still practiced regularly, when the workload allowed it.

She picked out the chords of one of her early songs and sang along, keeping her voice soft. "What's it gonna take to get you to notice? I've set my sights on you, come on you know this." So it wasn't Bob Dylan, but the kids had loved it back in the day. She'd heard it on the all-eighties satellite station not long ago and smiled at the memories it inspired.

A bongo beat accompanied the next verse and Randi stirred from her reverie to answer Kristy's call. "Bitch, where you been?"

A voice deepened by years of cigarettes laughed back. "Camping, in the effing rain. The one weekend it decides to pour cats and dogs in Southern California and we picked it. But we're home now." Kristy then faded for a few seconds while she gave a command to one of her grandkids. "You have a good birthday? I hope Gabby at least let you have the day off."

"If she had I wouldn't have taken it. I prefer spending my spare time here now," Randi said. It wasn't a lie. Despite what gossip sites reported, she relished the quiet, independent life. Besides, she'd seen and done plenty in her rock-and-roll days. She needed a decade or two to recover.

"When's your next hiatus? Zane and I miss you."

"Soon. I'll text you dates." She'd been meaning to visit the Porter clan in San Diego, though a part of her resisted. She had nothing against Kristy's domesticity, but when her friend started wheedling about her settling down, it made Randi want to hop on her bike and ride straight to Canada.

"You think you'd come up the first weekend of the month? There's going to be a mini-reunion of Snake Pit."

"Yeah?" Mini was the operative word. With Hal dead and ex-drummer Greg no longer performing, that left Zane and —

Kristy confirmed her suspicions. "Ian's new band is doing a show. It's not been publicized, but Zane's going to put in a special appearance at the encore."

Interesting. Randi thought back to Zane's post-Snake Pit career. He'd cut a few solo albums, neither of which had lived up to previous sales. His transition to scoring films had happened as a necessity when his voice had suffered a gradual decline. Hitting the high notes with Snake Pit had taken its toll, so if he planned to join Ian it meant he'd just play an instrument.

"Cool. You sure Ian won't be pissed if I'm there?" She'd forever recall the look on the guitarist's face when she'd smoked him in that impromptu guitar battle in San Bernardino. It sure wasn't awe he expressed.

Kristy snorted. "You always ask that when I mention getting together with him."

"Sue me. I prefer to keep as much awkward out of my life as possible."

"Liar."

Randi shrugged. "Well, if anybody else feels that way around me, it's not my problem."

Kristy laughed. "If Ian can remember that far back maybe he'll give you a pass, and I doubt he can so you're good." They enjoyed the crack, but after a few seconds it turned serious on the other side. "Listen," Kristy continued, "somebody else is coming, you should know."

"Oh-kay…" Randi tasted a sourness that settled in her gut. Kristy enjoyed setting her up on blind dates, but it seriously had to stop. Why ride all the way to San Diego to meet some boring old accountant neighbor friend of theirs? Again?

"Katharine Kushnirsky?" Kristy prodded, and Randi about burst with nostalgic joy.

"Kathy Lee Kush, and her neatly trimmed bush?" *So the male groupies praised, anyway.* "I haven't seen her in twenty years. She playing, too?"

"Rehearsing. She's in the lineup of a tour starting early next year, Ladies of the Eighties."

A chill shivered down Randi's breastbone. Funny how the subject of an oldies act tour came up after she'd touched on the same subject with Gabby. Randi should have expected to hear more of Kathy, though. Her fellow female rocker was enjoying a resurgence of fame thanks to the inclusion of her biggest hit in a recent blockbuster film. More than once Gabby had asked to use Randi's music on *Danse Macabre*, but she'd resisted the notion.

For one, she didn't own the rights to all her songs — the ones that made the real money. She got checks now and again for them, but not as much as she'd get if she owned them all. She'd be damned if she'd let the jackasses who held them make more money off her back.

She let out a long, whistling breath. Another chill rendered her immobile for a few seconds. She had a feeling...

"The promoter is looking for one more act," Kristy said. "Kathy's a draw, but they want another name."

"Subtlety was never your forte, Kris. Spill."

A deep sigh filled Randi's ear. "Derek is putting it together. Randi, this is perfect for you —"

Ugh. Ice hardened her heart and she almost hung up on her friend. She loved Kristy like a sister, but wanted to spit at the idea of her ex-manager manipulating the woman to get to her. "Kris," she warned, "we had an agreement. No mention of Derek unless it was the time and day of his funeral."

"Randi, it's been thirty years. You're not the same people anymore. At least hear him out."

That was why Kristy had invited her to San Diego. She doubted now Zane planned to perform with his old Snake Pit mate at all. "The only thing I want to hear from Derek Hynde is an admission that was he wrong. I bet he still can't do it."

Awkward silence turned Randi's mood, and she added in a softer voice, "Look, Kristy. I appreciate your calling, and I will come out to S.D. to see you guys. Maybe another time, 'kay?"

"Sure thing, Randi. Love you."

"Love you, too." Randi hung up and put her head on her desk.

* * * *

Derek watched the screen on Kristy's mobile change to indicate the ended call. He sat next to her husband, his former client, on the wicker loveseat opposite Kristy. Until this uncomfortable moment in time they had enjoyed a lovely evening on the Porters' back deck, which looked out over the Pacific Ocean. He'd come to the area to secure Kathy's place in the upcoming Ladies of the Eighties tour and had accepted Zane's invitation to dinner tonight.

Alas, Kristy's idea to persuade Randi into making a visit had fallen flat. He had expected as much. He and Randi had parted less than amicably all those years ago—and he was being kind as he remembered it. Randi, too. She'd managed to end the call without a string of creative curse words to describe him.

Planning his funeral, though, that hurt. Imagine if she had discovered he'd sat here the whole time, listening to her. Thank goodness the grandchildren staying overnight had just gone off to bed, or else they'd have learned a few new words from their Great-aunt Randi.

"It was kind of you to try, Kristy. Thank you," he said, rising to take his leave. "I suppose I'll talk to Jane, or

Rita. See if either of them are available to join the lineup."

"Jane just got inducted into the Hall of Fame. Can you afford her?" Zane joked as he escorted Derek to the door.

"You're implying Randi's cheaper?" The woman was priceless. Regardless of their relationship, or lack of one, his opinion of Randi's talent never wavered. It saddened him to know she hadn't performed her music in years, preferring a career in television. She reaped the praise and award nominations, yes, but Derek thought she belonged on stage, not behind a camera.

"I didn't mean that," Zane said. "Randi's great. Even when she was pissing me off and trying to make our band look bad." He laughed, then turned serious after a few seconds. "Look, I'm sorry if it put a damper on the evening—"

"Don't apologize. Everybody means well. I've come to accept the only thing that'll get Randi to agree to talk to me would be if she suffers amnesia." With a sad smile and shake of his head, Derek bade his friend good night and walked to his rental car.

The drive back to his hotel proved too short to clear his head, so rather than retire for the night, he opted for a drink in the lounge. With a seat on the terrace and a martini in hand, he settled before a dazzling view of lights reflecting on the bay. With one long look around the city he understood why the Porters and Kathy chose to call San Diego home. It seemed like an ideal place for him to retire if he didn't enjoy his work so much.

He had plenty of money, including residuals from what song rights he owned and wise investments over the years. A life spent managing various acts, however, yielded little time for a successful marriage, and he had no children. None he knew of, anyway. Unless that situation changed soon, he'd bequeath whatever he left to charity or Zane and Kristy's children, seeing as he was their godfather.

He sipped his drink as a thought of what might have been filled his head. Lost opportunities, wrong turns. A vision of a younger Randi Marsh glowed behind his eyes and he squeezed them shut to expel it.

She bloody well hates you. Decades after their last encounter and the sore feelings remained hard as granite. He'd let it happen, too. If only he'd said something, done something, when the fires between them had raged white hot.

Those memories heated him greater than the lighted firepit on the terrace.

Chapter Three

1984

"What's wrong with my hair?" Randi demanded. She patted the back of her head in a protective gesture and glared at the unsmiling consultant brought in to assist with her public image. Derek's colleague went by one name—"It's just Duncan," he'd said and offered a sideways glance of disapproval in lieu of a handshake—and wore tight white jeans with black vertical stripes and a red Oxford with every button fastened. Pointed-toe black boots completed the ensemble, and Randi cringed at the notion he might dress her in similar fashion.

"In a word, outdated." Duncan folded his arms tight against his chest and studied her with a critical eye, tut-tutting to himself every few seconds while shaking his head. The moments of silent disapproval embarrassed Randi. She might as well stand before the man in mismatched underwear. She understood the importance of a trendy appearance in this business, but with the way Duncan carried on it was as if he'd been charged to transform a Dickensian beggar child into the next rock goddess.

Randi touched her long, dirty-blonde locks. "I like my hair fine. I don't see why we have to change it."

"Sure, it's fine if you want to strum your banjo during Hootenanny Night at the Troubadour." Duncan rolled his eyes. "Derek wants you for the big time, girlie, and there's no room for hippie nostalgia." He twirled a forefinger in a command for Randi to turn in place for further inspection. "New clothes, new hair, new makeup. Well, some makeup…"

New sensations roiled in the pit of her stomach, an unease she'd never experienced. At least Duncan hadn't suggested she lose weight.

She'd come to the Los Angeles offices of Glissen Records, Snake Pit's label, at Derek's request. It meant skipping half of her classes, but as she neared graduation and had completed most of her year-end work, she'd managed to get free on the pretense of interviewing for a job. It wasn't quite a lie. Were Derek serious about his intent to launch and oversee a career for her in music, this counted.

The staff at Glissen had loaned Derek a meeting room, small and filled by a long conference table surrounded by swivel chairs. Duncan kept Randi in the most spacious corner while he clucked over her perceived drab appearance, never mind that she'd dressed in her best outfit—a pink silk blouse and gray designer pants with a matching jacket.

All the while Randi grew irritated and hoped it was worth waiting for Derek. *Where the hell did he go, anyway?* She swore, if Duncan moved to touch any part of her body she'd knee him in the crotch on her way to the exit.

"I don't suppose other artists go through this, huh?" she asked, ducking back a step when Duncan's finger appeared within poking distance of one breast. "You ever push a male singer into a room and nag him about his blue jeans?"

Duncan cocked a hip and rested his hand there. "Girlie, you should know this industry is dominated by men. They call the shots, they spend the marketing budget, and mostly on their own kind. Any woman foolish enough to keep up has to play the game to prove their worth."

"So…your answer is no?"

"I personally find the fashion sense of most top men's acts lacking, but put a white male musician in a business full of white men and I can assure you they get all the breaks and get to make up their own rules. If you're an inch as talented as Derek says, it won't be enough to impress the suits out there." He hooked his thumb toward the door, indicating the offices beyond them. "You know how the song from that musical goes? Dance ten, looks three?"

When Randi nodded, Duncan continued, "You're about at looks five right now. Got to be at least a nine-point-nine in the music video age."

Maybe this is a bad idea. "Funny, I thought my goal was to impress the people who buy records. I never cared what my favorite bands looked like."

Duncan snorted. "So you have no teen mag centerfolds of hunky rockers with hairy bare chests, wearing tight leather pants, plastered on your walls?"

Randi bristled, thinking for a moment of the life-sized likeness of her latest crush pinned to her closet door in all his sweaty, lusty glory. Then she lifted her chin at Duncan. "I've outgrown posters. That's more of a high school thing."

"Oh, you're not fooling me, girlie." Duncan arched an eyebrow. "I don't know what soda pop shop Derek plucked you from, but if you're smart you better —"

The consultant's warning went unsaid as the door opened and Derek, all professional in a dark suit and combed hair, entered with a smile.

She'd suffered enough, he decided. Derek watched through the window looking into the conference room as his would-be protegee interacted with Duncan. No sound filtered into the hallway, but he saw from her exasperated reactions how his friend rankled the young woman. Let it go another five minutes, and Derek guessed she'd escape and give no more thoughts to a life in music.

Not a good idea. Randi possessed a gift with the guitar, and soon she'd share it with the people who mattered, and who would help them through the next step.

He interrupted their conversation, noting a mask of relief on Randi's face as their gazes locked. "How's our new star, eh?"

"Stubborn," Duncan said.

"He wants to do stuff with my hair," Randi protested. "I don't mind wearing makeup or different clothes if it'll sway label execs, but can't I keep my hair the way I want it?"

Derek rocked on his heels, hands in pockets. Randi hoped to have him in her corner, he surmised, but Derek trusted Duncan's expertise. Over the years, the consultant had stayed on top of trends and transformed several acts managed by his father's firm, all for the better. He'd catch hell from Randi, for certain, but she was young. She had to put her faith in him.

Young being the operative term here. No way in hell had he bought her claim of being twenty-six. Thanks to a pal with connections in the state records department, he'd discovered Miranda Marsh wouldn't reach legal voting age for a few months yet. After they were through here, he had to convince at least one more person of her worth. Mom or Dad.

"I'm sure what Duncan has to suggest isn't as bad as all that," he said, hoping to placate both of them. "What? Some hairspray to give it some body."

"I want her to go platinum," Duncan cut in. "It's eye-catching, it photographs better, and it never goes out of style."

Randi touched her hair, eyes wide as though Duncan threatened to snatch the locks right off her head. "Not all singers are blondes. I can name a dozen and they've done just fine," she countered.

"I can't speak for them, but given the chance I'd definitely step in." Duncan moved toward the window and checked for activity on the other side. Derek tried not to smile at this act—his friend tended to wax dramatic when on the job. "Here's something you ought to know about the music business—insiders map out every move in advance. We plan the fads and the styles. You kids who buy the records might hear your favorite band is in the studio, but a hell of a lot more than music is being made." Another furtive glance toward the door caused Derek to check for spies as well.

"What is the big deal?" Randi asked, her expression weary. Duncan had them in a huddle now.

"In September there's going to be awards show for music videos," Duncan said.

"Well, duh. I've only seen promos for weeks."

"You haven't seen what will happen," Duncan snapped. "I have it on good authority from my friend Oliver, who knows a certain gentleman named Freddy, who manages a certain singer who likes to wear mesh and rosaries."

Derek saw it plain on Randi's face—the consultant had lost her. She was not impressed at all, giving both men a look that asked why she should be concerned about somebody who might turn out as a one-hit wonder.

"Her number for the awards ceremony, nobody's done anything like it before, and I guarantee you it will set tongues wagging. Ten years from now you won't remember who won what on the show, but you won't forget her. Ever." Duncan finished with a smug grin and a nod.

"Whatever." Randi let out a loud sigh. "So because of something she hasn't done yet, I have to color my hair?"

"Honey, if you're still here after September, you'll be demanding to use her stylist and I'll get to sing 'I told you so,'" Duncan trilled, much to Derek's amusement.

"Fat chance. Her music isn't bad, but I'm not a fan and I wouldn't want to emulate her." Randi shuddered and gave her full attention to Derek. "Can I go now? My parents are going to wonder why this is taking so long."

"Your parents?" He arched an eyebrow at her. "What have they to do with this?"

Aha. He wanted to smile, having caught her slip, but toned down the smug when Randi flushed a deep red. Rather than call her out on her minority, he waited for the next lie. This wasn't the time or place for humiliation. Randi had to bring her A-game to Glissen.

"Not that it's any of your business, but I'm meeting them for dinner later." She gave a hair flip and a withering glance. "It's something we do once a week."

Well, not a complete untruth, he surmised.

"That's very sweet, love. I'll make sure you're not late for your engagement. We just have an informal audition to get through. Nothing major," he added on seeing her eyes widen. "I want you to play and sing like you did for me the other night."

"I-I didn't bring my guitar. I didn't think I had to, I thought this was a meeting."

"It's a record label, love. They have to hear what you offer. Don't worry, I have a guitar set up for you."

They bade Duncan farewell and he led Randi down the hallway toward a larger conference room, where the highest-ranking executives of the label waited, no doubt checking their watches and tapping with impatience. Derek stole a glance at his charge, worrying for the first time today. Fear seemed to project from her small frame. He'd managed to get this far thanks to his father's name. He required Randi to stay cool for the rest of the trip.

"My grandmother died of cancer," she said, her voice low.

"Today?" *Bloody hell.*

She let out a stiff laugh. "Last year. Bone cancer, spread to her brain. She'd gotten her hair done once a week for decades. Mom said it was probably the chemicals that did it..." Randi's voice cracked and Derek then understood her reluctance to yield all the way with Duncan. She'd wear a sleazy outfit, okay, because thong underwear didn't make people sick.

"We can discuss that later, love. Besides, I doubt you'd have much upkeep with one dye job."

"I haven't signed any papers yet. You can't force a makeover on me," she said.

"Let's win over these suits first, eh? You secure a deal with your rendition of *Highway Star* and you can wear your hair any way you want it. Shave it all off, if you care."

She laughed. "Yeah, like that look will work for anybody." After a beat, "Was he serious back there about that video awards number becoming the next big thing? There's better singers out there."

"There's a better singer standing next to me, and Duncan is rarely wrong about things. He knows she'll be big and you as well."

Randi frowned. "He said nothing to me about it."

"He stayed with you while I was away. That's how I know. Duncan wouldn't have bothered with you otherwise."

He rapped his knuckles on the door and waited for the invitation to enter. She walked into the room as Derek gestured her toward their destiny.

* * * *

Randi watched the scenery blur past from the passenger seat of the sports car Derek drove east on I-210 toward home. She chewed on the straw plunged into the chocolate milkshake procured for her via a drive-thru stop, and processed the past hour or so of her life. She'd stood before a semi-circle of seated suits, not a one under the age of sixty and all unsmiling and whistling through their noses as they breathed. Without direction, she had picked up the guitar attached to a portable amp in their midst and recreated her impromptu concert as done in Snake Pit's green room. That time, however, she'd extended the set to include a hard-driving instrumental and had been halfway through a classic rockabilly tune when she'd spotted Derek's cutting-throat gesture.

The suits had murmured to each other. She'd leaned against Derek for support and pressed her hand to her chest to calm her heart's wild beat. Minutes later, the man with the most hair and least crooked teeth had stood and informed Derek to expect contracts at his father's California office.

Bada bing, bada boom. A record label wanted to sign her, and she was sitting in a fancy car with a man intent on making fame happen. A man, she realized, she didn't know very well. She had questions. For starters...

"Why do you have a car? I thought you were getting by on a tour bus with Snake Pit?"

Derek assumed a casual position as he drove, right hand on the wheel and the left leaning on the open driver's side window. In his mirrored sunglasses, he projected a rather mysterious persona, not unlike a British film spy.

Not a bad looking one at that.

He tilted his head toward her. "It's on loan from a friend, love. Black Alchemy have a few dates in the area, and I don't have to babysit Snake Pit twenty-four-seven. They might act like sods, but they're grown men with some sense."

"Seems kind of weird to have a show in San Bernardino and then the next one in L.A. We're an hour apart, so why not have people drive in to one place?"

"For starters, we intended to do three dates in Los Angeles, but the venue didn't have three consecutive nights open. We settled on San Bernardino since it was on the way from Las Vegas, where we were prior to all this."

Good answer. Seeing as she'd come into this conversation with little knowledge of the business, it made some sense to her. "What happens after I sign all the agreements you gave me?" She patted the stack of papers lodged between her seat and the center console. What legalese she'd glimpsed before they'd set off for home had left her head spinning. She hoped her friend Tina's brother, a pre-law student, had time to interpret it for her.

"Then we plan. We figure out songs for you to record, find a studio to do work, discuss marketing with the label. So much to take care of." Derek turned to her with a flashing smile before returning his attention to the road.

"How do you intend to oversee my career while you're on the road with Snake Pit?"

"I won't be. When it's morning in London I'm calling my father to tell him I will assign one of his juniors in the California office to take my place on tour."

"You can do that?"

"You ask a lot of questions."

Randi shrugged and stared at the road. "This is going to be my life, so I want to know what I'm in for. Everything's already second nature for you. I don't like surprises. I want to be prepared."

More than that, she wanted to be eighteen, of legal age to agree to any proposals on her own. All through the drive home, she worried over her parents' reaction to her deceit. Randi knew they had hoped she might at least attend a community college for an associate's degree, or get some kind of certification to help her into a decent job with benefits. Her grades weren't the best, but she'd graduate, and the idea of punching a clock to work as somebody's secretary made her skin crawl.

What Derek was offering her—a chance to play guitar for a living—seemed like a dream. Her father, in particular, had long championed her talent, but Randi knew if he got his hands on these contracts he'd insist on dissecting every clause.

Maybe saying no, insisting she was too young.

If she signed them on her own, building on the lie about her being twenty-six, would she get into legal trouble down the road? Randi wondered how long she'd be able to keep up her boost in age.

She pointed out her exit to Derek and guided him to her neighborhood. To her relief, she saw no cars parked in the driveway, which meant she'd beaten her parents' home.

"Thanks again for the ride." She unclipped her seat belt, happy to soon unfold herself from this compact car. "It was nice of you to come all this way."

"Not a problem, love. The idea of you riding on a bus for hours, especially after you came to L.A. in one…" His face twisted with disgust.

"It's okay. I had a nap on the trip up, and it's not like it's a city bus. I took the Greyhound." With one eye open, she recalled. The old lady sitting next to her that morning had leered at her purse with great interest.

"Well, I hope you get your car repairs sorted out before the next meeting." He nodded toward the empty driveway, and Randi bit her lip. *That's right.* She'd told Derek she rented this house on her own and the car required a new belt of some kind.

"In fact," he added, "once all the papers are signed, you ought to consider moving closer for your convenience. It won't do to commute so far every day."

"I'll let you know. Uh, rent is much cheaper here. Anyway, thanks again and I'll wait for your call." She took the sheaf of contracts and got out to prevent him from extending the conversation and risking a slip-up in her story to him. She unlocked the front door and stepped inside, then waited in the living room for his car to roll away.

"Close one," she murmured, and relaxed. After a few seconds, she heard panting and small footsteps pounding on the carpet, and she crouched low to hug her yellow Lab, Buster. "How you doing, sweetie? You been a good boy today?" Buster barked his assent and Randi laughed. "Yeah, I'm sorry I wasn't here right after school. I had some important business in the big city. Yes, I did." She tilted her face to take the brunt of Buster's licking on her chin and neck, then straightened and walked toward the kitchen for snacks all around.

She took an apple for herself and grabbed a bone-shaped treat for Buster. It occurred to her that when she moved out of the house — regardless of what happened with Derek and Glissen Records — her parents might lobby to keep the dog. Buster had come to them when Randi was eleven, and she'd understood he was her dog, but of course her parents also loved him. Would they argue for him staying behind due to his age, or assume whatever apartment Randi found wouldn't take pets?

Once she recorded an album, she'd be expected to tour to support it. Would Derek allow Buster on a tour bus? "Damn," she muttered. *How come I didn't think about these things?*

In her room, she dropped the papers on her desk, then flung herself on her bed and stared at the ceiling for a minute. Posters of her idols covered almost every inch of the walls. She'd procured a number of them from the local record store where a friend worked — she got the promotional items destined for the trash when the new décor arrived. Not every face staring back at her was a rock star, either. A few actors and models were represented, but her room served as her own personal hall-of-fame exhibit.

She grabbed her acoustic guitar, positioned her left fingers on a fret and strummed a chord. As much as she loved the powerful drive of a rock solo, she appreciated the beauty of a guitar's natural sound. When she had first asked her parents for a guitar, they'd relented on the condition she start with classical lessons. This, despite her father's shared love for rock. When she could perform a few standards with some degree of competency they would spring for heavier machinery, they'd promised. Randi figured out she was being tested — her parents weren't about to spend money if she wasn't serious about music.

She'd mastered a number of Spanish pieces and a few pop-tinged, easy-listening hits which had gone over well with the intellectual set her parents entertained on occasion. To Randi's relief, it wasn't a distant leap from Getz and Gilberto to Lennon, McCartney and Tony Iommi.

Randi found it funny, her parents' desire to keep up snooty appearances. Her father kept his love for the hard stuff hidden in public. It pleased his patrician wife, Randi supposed, but what was the harm in cutting loose once in a while?

So she played classical and modern very well, and now it was time for the next step as suggested by Derek — songwriting. The suits at Glissen seemed to enjoy her renditions of established acts, but what else did she bring to the table? Randi had thought to expect the label to pitch her songs from some hit factory, but on the ride home Derek had insisted she try to write her own. "You'll get more money up front," he'd said, "and as long as you own the rights, you'll have a near perpetual cash flow."

Not news for her. She'd studied the legalities of music rights with the same enthusiasm as she pursued her talent. She was a scholar of rock and roll, but not creative writing.

She picked through a melody for a few more minutes before setting down her guitar and reaching for a notebook. Whenever a line or usable thought came to her, she jotted it down. But with no organizational pattern to her scribblings, the whole thing looked like a long, incomprehensible train of babble. Randi turned to a fresh page and let her mind clear of doubt. "What kind of songs do they want?" Nobody had advised her at the meeting—they'd just offered her a deal and shooed her and Derek out of the door in order to phone conference with Japan.

Central themes of her favorite tunes came to mind. Love, partying, sex, fulfillment of desires, ego. Randi hated to brag about herself, stayed home most nights and remained a virgin. *Who wants to hear a song about that?*

She checked her watch to find she had at least an hour before one parent or the other came home. Plenty of time to blast some tunes and wait for inspiration. Rolling onto her stomach, she crawled across her bed, stretched for the bookcase near her stereo and selected a few tapes. Buster whined his disapproval at his mistress' song choice and, when she made no move to switch to something more pleasing to him, loped away.

"Everybody's a critic," she called after the dog, then leaned back on her pillow and closed her eyes. The one disadvantage to this, no way to write in the dark. So she sat up, grabbed the notepad on her bedside table and began a free-form word association game as the guitars screeched from her speakers.

Dreams, hopes, life, beauty, starry nights and cold drinks to quench hot tempers...she filled a few pages with words but none of them seemed to fit together. She thought of the women in rock preceding her on this journey. One hit big with a few cover songs, and Randi wondered if Glissen would have her do the same. The others sang about men who did them wrong, men who tempted them from home, men she surmised they knew well. No such luck for her.

Well, there was her father, the man who encouraged her endeavors yet wasted no time in warning her off some of her ambitions. He'd had dreams as well, she imagined, but had opted for the safety of college, the job with benefits and the nice girl who won his parents' approval.

He played it safe, and Randi loved him and sometimes felt bad he never left his comfort zone.

She tapped her pencil on her lower lip. Something popped in her brain, like crackling candy. *Play it safe. Play it safe, daddy warned me...be a good girl, come on home.*

Disjointed words became lyrics. Lyrics stretched into stanzas. By the time a door slammed in the distance Randi had finished her first song.

She held up the pad to view the finished draft, swelling with pride. It pained her to write essays for English, but this came so easy to her. She'd take this to Derek to see what he thought of it, get his input on setting it to music.

A short rap on her door diverted her attention, and she set the pad face down on her table as her father entered.

"Hey, honey bunches. How was the interview?" Steven Marsh leaned in the doorway and exchanged a smile with her. Randi looked at him and, as she often had, marveled at his youthful good looks. She'd gotten her eye and hair color from him, and hoped for more of his genes, especially the ones that slowed age.

Of course, her father seldom spent time in the sun and ate no meat. Playing it safe. *You'll look good, but what memories do you take from it?*

"It went okay, I guess," she said, glancing down to keep from betraying herself.

"Who was it for again, that insurance group who called last week?"

"Yeah," she lied. "I don't expect anything to come from it."

"That's fine. Good to have a few practice runs under your belt, and there's still Valley College." Steven turned toward her table, staring at her stacked books and papers with interest. Randi held her breath.

Shit, the contracts. She cut her gaze to her desk on the other side of the room. Steve paid the furniture no mind.

"You finish all that paperwork for it?" he asked.

"Last week." She'd filled out everything, anyway. Dad hadn't asked if she'd mailed it.

The phone rang, and Randi sagged with silent relief when her father strolled toward the kitchen to answer. If whomever had called disrupted him enough to put an end to their awkward third degree about academics and jobs, she'd be grateful. She sprang from the bed and placed a book on top of the paper stack, then took the pad and tore away the sheet containing her song, unsure of why she wanted to hide it from him. If she called it poetry, he might encourage her to write more, or else critique what she'd composed so far.

Derek needed to read it first, she decided. He was the expert in the business.

Her dad reappeared, not concealing some disappointment. "Well, kiddo, looks like your mother's working late tonight."

"Again?" *Third time this week.* Randi guessed Mom's relief had gone MIA and Cindy Marsh had to sit tight until her manager found somebody to cover the next shift.

"It happens." Steven sighed. "It's also why you have to make sure you turn in all those forms."

"Yeah." She knew the speech by heart. Turn in the forms. Get the degree. Get a job that doesn't require a nametag pinned to your breast. *Right.* A framed certificate on her wall guaranteed nothing.

"At this rate, we might as well move our things into the office so we can be a family again," she said.

"Funny. I'll get the tofu Pad Thai and vegan Tom Yum for two." Where they ordered, it was enough to feed the three of them. That settled, her dad winked at her and disappeared.

"Don't forget the spring rolls!" Randi called to the darkened hallway, then settled back in bed. She let the renewed silence envelop her as she closed her eyes and sang her lyrics in her head.

> *Play it safe, Daddy warned me*
> *Be a good girl, come on home*
> *But baby did me wrong, he scorned me*
> *That's why right now, I need to roam.*

"Man, that sucks," she whispered. Okay, so songwriting came easier to others. It was the first draft, too, so no reason to trash it just yet. Maybe going most of the day on an empty stomach stifled her creativity. She'd eat Thai food, watch the prime-time game shows with her dad then try another song when her mom came home. Her parents often spent their evenings with wine and conversation, leaving Randi the peace required for her work.

Still, with little to no experience in romantic entanglements…it stood to threaten her productivity. She either had to pick up a few romance novels for inspiration, or find a willing guy to help her out.

Or a girl. Randi had come to accept her romantic feelings weren't limited to one gender, but she doubted the music world was ready for that kind of song. Not with the AIDS crisis happening and inspiring so much homophobia.

She thought of Derek, handsome and professional and way older than she. She bet he had a date tonight with a bikini model or bit actress, somebody to escort backstage at the Black Alchemy show. What would it be like to go out with somebody like him? Dinner at some fancy Beverly Hills joint, followed by a moonlit drive into the Hills in his car… Randi let her fantasy take shape in her mind, and dreamed of being able to do the same thing one day. She'd sell a million records and afford many nights like that.

And perhaps one night treat Derek to dinner and hope he accepted.

* * * *

His instincts paid off. After a leisurely drive around the block to convince Randi he'd returned to L.A., Derek parked several houses down from hers and waited. About twenty minutes later, he saw the man he presumed to be her father turn onto the driveway, then contemplated his next move. He knew contacts able to get personal information from Mr. Marsh's license plate. Derek thought of how he might approach the man at his workplace, when Mr. Marsh exited the house for his car and backed up the street.

Derek put his car into drive. "Off to the pub to hoist a few, then?" He longed for a stout himself, but swallowed his disappointment when he followed the blue sedan into a parking lot abutting a Thai restaurant. Spicy food tore up his stomach every time he tried it. *Mr. Marsh must be getting dinner for the family to go.*

He hung back at the entrance, watching as his mark exchanged a few words with the hostess and took a seat at the bar to wait. While he opened a checkbook to pay, Derek slid onto the next stool and signaled the bartender for the one draft choice that appealed most.

"I'll never get used to these so-called 'pints,'" he groused on seeing the smallish glass set before him. At least it was happy hour. He caught Randi's father's eye and smiled, raising his drink. "Cheers, mate."

The man nodded back. "If you're looking for something more like home, there's a great pub in Redlands. Not far."

"It's good. I prefer to live like the locals when I travel. Thought tonight I needed a change from bean sprouts and quiche." The man's chuckling encouraged him, and Derek held out his hand. "Derek Hynde."

"Steven Marsh."

"Yes, you're Randi's father."

So much for the good feelings. Steven's face darkened into a protective father mask, his eyes asking why and how a man who appeared close to thirty knew his teenage daughter.

Derek figured talking fast served the best chance of getting heard. He reached into his pocket for a business card and a cassette. "I'm with JZD Entertainment. I represent musicians, and your daughter auditioned for me today—"

"No, you must be mistaken," Steve cut him off. "My daughter said nothing to me about meeting an entertainment manager. She isn't one to lie."

Care to bet, mate? Well, maybe she omitted some details. "Mr. Marsh, I wouldn't have attempted to meet you if Randi hadn't delivered a stellar guitar performance for me and executives with Glissen Records." Steven arched an eyebrow and he continued, "If I may be so bold as to speculate, Randi's age is a deciding factor where her musical career is concerned. It would explain her reluctance to tell you of her whereabouts today."

"Since when does Randi have a musical career? She's in high school."

"I'm sorry, but she graduates rather soon, yes?"

Steven ripped the check for his order from its pad with a bit of force. Derek noticed a tear in the ragged edge. "Be that as it may, she's still seventeen and unable to agree to any contract without parental permission." Derek winced at the sharp look directed at him. "I don't know JZD Entertainment from a hole in the ground. How do I know you're not some pervert with fake business cards out to get my girl? I've worked in the business in the past, Mr. Hynde, and I've seen what it does to young people."

Well, that came as news to Derek, but he'd dug only so deep into the Marsh family for information. Knowing this inspired doubt in his mind, as he recalled relationships with people in the business who swore Hollywood would never have their children. "What sort of business are you in, Mr. Marsh, if I might ask?"

"Cameraman. I worked for a number of network shows before I got married and moved out here. Now I'm with the local station, on the morning shows and midday news so I can be home for Randi."

"And Mrs. Marsh?"

"Emergency dispatcher." Steven looked up, as though thinking of a British equivalent. "You know, people dial nine-one-one…"

"Yes, we have something similar back home." He'd availed himself of the American version once, too, when a client had passed out after binge drinking. Derek turned toward the bar and noticed a boom box lodged in between some bottles. He motioned for the bartender with the cassette pinched in his fingers. "Excuse me, do you mind if we borrow that for a second?"

He said to Steven, "I want you to listen to your daughter's performance and hear the professionalism and raw talent. I don't know if you're musically inclined, Mr. Marsh, but having seen Randi play guitar I am convinced she has a future as a recording artist. I'm not just saying it because she's young and pretty."

The bartender set up the tape, and Steven mumbled, "Young and pretty gets too many girls in trouble."

"I would protect Randi like she was my own daughter. I don't expect you to believe me, but I am willing to offer you full transparency where her relationship with my firm is concerned."

Soon, voices erupted from the portable stereo's built-in speakers. Derek's voice introduced Randi, who said hello, then announced her audition song. Seconds later the locomotive-drive of a heavy metal hit rose in volume and Randi's voice flowed into the space. Derek relished the way Steven's face softened and mouth gaped as he listened.

"That's Randi?" her father asked.

Derek nodded.

"By herself? She wasn't backed by a group there?" At the second nod, Steven slumped a bit in his stool. "She practices every night, I know that, and she's played a few songs for us and friends. That was just fooling around and having a good time, though. This here—" he gestured to the boom box—"that's amazing."

"You see why a label wants to sign her, Mr. Marsh? Randi has the potential to become a major artist." Derek leaned forward. "She needs good representation, and I can do that for her."

Steven cut him a sharp glance. Derek deflated. *Not quite yet, eh?*

"Potential is one thing, staying power is another. You seem so enthusiastic about her now, but what happens when the next wunderkind comes along and you dump Randi on the side of the road?" The look in the older man's eyes told Derek what Steven might commit to if Derek reneged on promises to his daughter.

"That's why I drew up a contract that outlines what our firm expects of Randi and what we'll give her." Derek crooked his head toward the door. "It's in my car and I'll give it to you to read. Randi can't sign on her own, being underage, and I don't expect she'd wait to turn eighteen when Glissen Records wants to work with her now."

Steven said nothing for a minute. Behind them, a server approached and set a large paper bag by the older man's elbow. Derek asked for his tape back and Randi's father seemed to wake from a reverie when the music stopped.

He grabbed the bag and stepped down from his seat. "Mr. Hynde, I'll walk you to your car," he said.

Chapter Four

Present Day

"What's his story?"

Randi looked up from her desk to see Jessie, Too True's receptionist, standing close and shuffling the incoming mail. She hadn't heard the young woman enter, and Jessie's unannounced presence just about seized her heart. Randi despised stealth surprises like this—it reminded her of stories involving colleagues attacked by stalker fans. She decided to gift Jessie something with a bell attached—maybe a necklace of tiny tinkling cymbals—to help warn people she was approaching.

Yeah, why not? It would match Jessie's hippie-dippie wardrobe. Randi leaned to one side and noted the girl had shucked off her flats. It would explain her extra-sneaky abilities today.

"What's whose story?" she asked, and set down the guitar she'd been strumming.

"That guy who was just here in your office." Jessie handed her two envelopes.

"Oh, Barry?" Randi shrugged. "He looked bored sitting up front with nothing to do, so I thought I'd cheer him up."

"He came with Steffi."

"No shit? He must get around." She knew this. Barry had revealed his story to her when she'd found him in the lobby earlier, perched like a tense dental patient. Randi chuckled, thinking of the first time she'd met the aforementioned Barry Spahn. He'd been a seat filler at a recent major television awards ceremony, a volunteer with zero benefits who'd no doubt gotten duped by a desperate event planner. In a moment of serendipity, he'd ended up next to Randi for the last twenty or so minutes of the live broadcast, and Randi—well aware of the rigid rules imposed upon the poor guy—had flirted like a coquette and tempted him to crack. Barry had wound up as part of the onstage celebration when *Danse Macabre* won the Best Drama award, and played an important role in an ensuing viral moment.

Aside from that, his admission that he aspired to write for the screen, and this news about his leaving with Steffi, was all she knew about the man. Randi figured as much—most handsome people she encountered in L.A. wanted some role to play in the business, if not acting then something close to her job. Well, she wasn't ready to retire yet.

She also wrote for shit—TV dialogue, anyway. If Gabby's plans for her came to fruition, it made her responsible for finding writers. It seemed unlikely the staff at *Danse Macabre* would defect. Barry had seemed eager to help.

"Gabby not tell you?" Jessie pressed. "It's all over town about Steffi losing her driver's license. I heard he's a rideshare driver hired to take her places." She clicked her tongue in sympathy. "Can you imagine having to chauffeur her everywhere?"

"She's not the devil, give her a break."

Gabby's voice startled Jessie enough to cause the young woman to squeal. Gabby filled the open doorway, folded her arms and cut a stern, disapproving stare. "You think it's possible to be nice to Steffi Corden for the duration of her story arc? She's had a rough few months, and it's harder to cope when the whole world knows your troubles."

"Sorry," Jessie mumbled, contrite. She handed Gabby the rest of the mail and padded away, leaving the producer and the director to exchange sighs.

"For what it's worth, I'm willing to give her the benefit of the doubt," Randi said. "I know what it's like to be down and out and grateful as all hell for a second chance." She'd never watched *ViP*, Steffi's show with ExStream, but knew the actress by reputation. Her recent public tantrums aside, the woman took her craft seriously. Randi considered a future working with Steffi on *Fallen Angel*, the proposed *Danse Macabre* spinoff to star Steffi's guest-star character...if the network greenlighted it.

We shall see. Randi got to keep her office in the Too True building regardless of what happened, but the idea of working on a different TV show felt to her like an unwanted work transfer. Not just that, but with *Fallen Angel* her title changed to showrunner. It meant calling every shot and making sure nobody goofed off on company time.

So who watches the boss to see that she doesn't fool around?

"Have you eaten yet?" Gabby asked her. "I know it's not quite lunch but I'm starving."

"Sure, I guess." Randi eyed the closed lower-left drawer of her desk, where her unappetizing PB and J and a bruised apple waited for her. A burrito and margarita from the Tex-Mex place down the street seemed like an awesome tradeoff. *Extra guac, please.* "I thought you packed one today, though?" She recalled Gabby saying something about wanting to eat better.

"I did. I ate it." She laughed. "I made my own lunch today and even though I had a bagel for breakfast I was still hungry. So now I have to buy lunch to replace the one I had for second breakfast."

Randi stood and patted her front pockets to check for her phone and credit card wallet. She never carried a purse, not since high school. "Maybe we ought to go in one of those subscription snack boxes. Non-GMO trail mix and dried fruit, that kind of stuff?"

"I'd eat everything in it, and the cardboard box it came in." Gabby frowned. "I don't know what's come over me lately."

"Stress," Randi said. *Been there, done that.* "We won all those awards and now we have to top ourselves in the new season. No pressure." She rolled her eyes, then barked out a laugh. "C'mon, let's get margaritas." The mere thought of daytime drinks lifted her mood.

They left her office to find Jessie heading their way, a voluminous display of yellow roses concealing her face.

"Whoa." Randi turned to Gabby. "Okay, what'd Dash do to require an apology like this?"

"Actually, these are for you." Jessie handed over the green column vase and made to reach for the tiny card on its plastic pitchfork, but Randi jerked it out of her reach. "I guess it's a late birthday present," the receptionist added, sounding a tad miffed.

"Weird." Randi held the bouquet at arm's length. Flowers as a gift was foreign to her. *What goofball thinks this would be an ideal present for Randi Marsh, the wild child of TV drama?* A true friend might have sent her passes to a rock festival or a new front spoiler for her motorcycle.

"Don't keep us in suspense, Randi. Who sent them?" Gabby asked. She eyed the card as if she might eat it after opening, and as Randi was just as curious to know she stepped to the closest table to keep from dropping the heavy glass. She opened the little envelope to reveal a business card-sized greeting, handwritten against an embossed floral design, and her heart squeezed hard.

Free for lunch at Jerry's? Hoping to bury the hatchet under a plate of cheese fries.
Love, D –

Underneath that was a mobile number to RSVP. The corners of the card pinched the pads of her thumb and forefinger and her mouth went dry.

"Is that the famous 'D' we're not allowed to mention?" Gabby was looking over her shoulder. Jessie, standing on the other side of her, watched with saucer eyes – all the wider to absorb this popcorn-munching moment.

"I won't know for certain because I have no intention of calling or texting or meeting anybody at Jerry's." Randi tossed the card next to the vase. Gabby snatched it.

"Go."

"No," Randi snapped.

"See what he has to say," Gabby insisted. "You haven't seen him in over twenty years, right? Who holds a grudge for that long?"

I can think of someone. Nevertheless, Randi bit her tongue. She loved Gabby too much to needle her about her estranged parents, two of the most overbearing people Randi had encountered in her life. The Randalls, formerly Gabby's managers, had derailed Gabby's first marriage to Dash Gregory many years ago, all for the sake of an acting career the woman no longer wanted. These days they were semi-retired, but Randi caught their names in the trades on occasion, connected to child actors contracted to projects. Gabby refrained from communicating with them, but once in a while the couple crashed crew get-togethers in town, allowing Randi to experience their pushiness first hand.

"I understand your curiosity, Gabby, but really…he's the past and I prefer to leave all that behind me."

"If you're worried about things getting tense or ugly, I'll go there with you for support."

"I wanna come, too," Jessie piped up. She punctuated her interest with a tight-fisted, girl-power salute.

No, no, no. Not ending up as a screech owl, bawling out her ex-manager, on the hippie chick's social media.

Randi stepped closer to the main entrance, putting space between her and the flowers. *What a weak gift to accompany an olive branch,* she decided. She deserved a gold watch or a suitcase of unmarked bills from Derek, not a flippant note attached to something liable to die when she returned from lunch.

"Derek doesn't intimidate me," she said, and cringed. Well, she'd gone and said his name out loud. Two more times in front of a mirror and she'd summon a demon. "He's a part of my life that ended. I move forward."

"Yet you still hang out with Zane Porter and Greg Orville," Gabby said. The knife twisted.

"You hush. They're not assholes. Anymore."

"We'll come in five minutes after you and sit in a back booth. He doesn't have to know," Jessie said.

"You hush too."

All went silent as Randi stormed into her office for her helmet. When she returned, Gabby and Jessie were sitting on the lobby sofa, watching her with a mixture of sympathy and urgency. Randi pondered the chances of them letting this go after today, which seemed low if Derek continued to send peace offerings and invitations.

Two grown women with the potential to turn into petulant children, asking 'are we there yet' every five seconds until she cracked... She'd never get any work finished.

She sighed. "Look, I'll go to Jerry's and hear him out. Doesn't mean I'll forgive him for doing me wrong or agree to anything he wants. I'm ordering the most expensive thing they have and sticking him with the check. Be good and I'll have him spring for black-and-white cookies for the whole office."

She was out of the door as Jessie muttered, "I hope a guy sends me flowers when I'm sixty."

"Oh, honey," Randi whispered, fastening her helmet. "Me too, I guess."

* * * *

The circular corner booth in the back used to be theirs. It sat up to five, but at the peak of Randi's musical career the deli staff had seen no harm in allowing the latest rock sensation and her manager to enjoy some seclusion and elbow room. Derek tended to tip enough for five diners, anyway.

At one point, they'd hung a signed eight by ten of Randi on the wall there. It was a face shot, her hair sprayed and teased into a hundred bleached spikes around her head, her eyelids dark with three shadows and lips pursed to kiss. Sitting here now, the place nearly deserted, Derek glanced at what had replaced the photo. An actor—or singer or whatever—he'd never heard of, wearing a tux, smirked down at him. The black marker platitude and signature scrawled across the glossy were damn near illegible.

No sense in trying to decipher it, Derek decided as he grabbed his menu. So much had changed since the last time he had eaten here. They offered different sandwiches, and more hot plates...at three times what he used to pay. No more New York-style seltzers and draft root beer, either, just regular soft drinks. Only the rotating display tower up front with its thick cheesecakes and glazed-fruit tortes looked like it withstood progress. That, and Derek's memories.

Randi was born again in this very booth. Derek thought back to that day.

"What do you think of Delilah?" he asked, pen poised over a paper napkin.

Randi sipped her egg cream. "Who's she?"

"She's you." Randi's eyes grew big and she coughed a bit. He added, "Your stage name. I'm trying to come up with a good one here."

"How about Randi Marsh? There's nothing wrong with my name, and I'm the one who's going to be singing and playing. Why shouldn't I get the credit?"

"It's not about giving credit to somebody else, love. Part of it is privacy, so you can have something of a normal life when

you're not performing. Also…well, the suits at Glissen don't feel Randi Marsh is a marketable enough name."

"I can think of a few rock star names that don't sound marketable."

Derek ignored that. "I bet they're not with Glissen, love. Anyway, something short, easy to remember – alliteration is good. Like your Kathy Kush. She just had her second top ten hit, you know."

"Fine, so we'll use my full name. Miranda Marsh. That alliterate enough for you?"

He shook his head. "Sounds too formal, love. Sorry." She sighed and blew bubbles into her drink while he pondered. "I fear even if we keep Randi people will think you borrowed it from Randy Rhoads." He thought about the guitar player who had died in a horrific plane crash a few years prior.

"Only if I start calling myself Rhoads, too," she said. "I haven't recorded one song yet and already I've agreed to change my hair, my face and my clothes. Can I least keep my first name?"

There was no letting this go, but Derek understood. She wanted some part of her identity to keep her grounded. "Very well. What's a good word that starts with R? Bear in mind, love, where I come from 'randy' means horny, so no animals."

Two egg creams later, they'd settled on Raucous as her professional surname. Randi considered it the least ridiculous of the choices given her, but at least it looked good done up in a lightning bolt font on the cover of her first LP.

"I hope you ordered the express lunch. It's about all I have time for."

Her voice broke through his reverie, coarser now than thirty years ago. Maybe a combination of age and various vices — hell if he knew — but in his eyes Randi still looked amazing, younger than her true age and the one the world believed. She wore no makeup and bound her hair in a sloppy ponytail, and it appeared her taste in clothing had changed little over the years. Rock band T-shirt, black jeans, shit-kicker boots.

"You must have stepped through a time warp, love." He stood to greet her, but she waved him back down without touching him, then sat as opposite from him in the booth as possible. *Disappointing.*

"Look past me and see if two women are here hiding behind menus," she ordered.

"Well, hello to you as well."

Randi sighed. "Derek, you know I don't want to be here—"

"Yet here you are, love." He wanted to smile as she cringed. The endearment continued to rankle her. Cute, but he hadn't come to twist any invisible knives. "For what it's worth, I'm glad you showed. Happy belated birthday."

"Thanks."

Derek fingered the small velvet box in his suit coat pocket. Nothing fancy, just a miniature charm of a rhinestone studded guitar one wore on a chain. Randi had never been much for jewelry, but in his memory she wore different pendants over the years. Gemstones, guitar picks, gifts from fans. Today, he noticed a silver locket around her neck.

"That looks nice," he said, nodding toward it. "Antique?"

Randi fingered the curled etchings on the oval shape and shrugged. "No. Gabby gave me this last Christmas." She pried it open to reveal photos of her late parents.

"Ah." He let go of the box and folded his hands on the table. Something told him now wasn't the time for more presents. Randi fumed in her seat, offering one-word answers and blunt phrases when prompted. She smiled once for the waiter who came to take their order. After he set down Derek's diet soda and her egg cream, she leaned forward and scowled.

"What do you want?"

"To treat you to lunch," he said. "Despite our history, I still consider you a friend, Randi. You had a birthday and I want to celebrate it with you."

"That can't be all of it, Derek. You're a businessman first, and you've had twenty chances at birthdays to buy me food. Just because we haven't spoken in years doesn't mean you've changed. I see your name pop up online."

"If you mean I'm still in management, then yes." He pulled long on his soda can. "I do hope to talk business with you, but we have time for that yet."

"I'm not quitting my job."

"I'm not asking you to."

"I also don't set my own hours, Derek. I don't have the luxury of two-hour Hollywood lunches. I have to be back at the office soon."

Derek chuckled. "Oh, surely if you're running late Gabby would stroll up here to let you know."

Randi turned to look behind her, the direction where Derek had smiled and waggled his fingers. Gabby Randall and some other girl were squeezed onto the same bench of a far booth, facing them. The second Randi's head turned they hid behind giant plastic menus.

She returned her attention to him, shaking her head. A smile came close to breaking out but she tamped it back with a sip of her drink.

Her reaction encouraged him. He wanted to massage that good mood for what he planned next. "We had some good talks in this booth, long ago." He spoke in a wistful voice, hoping she'd take the cue and contribute. "I learned you were quite sharp with your music history."

Randi took the bait, to his great pleasure. "I remember a lot of arguments in this booth, most of which I won. Especially the one about my stage name." She shuddered.

"Yes, I dare say you were right all along there. You weren't suited as a Delilah. Imagine, too, if you had gone by Fuchsia Fox."

"She rocks all day, and Fox all night." Randi snorted, and tapped out a rimshot on the tabletop.

"Shame they took your picture down." Derek glared at the photo of the starlet occupying that space. "No need to replace you."

"Not replaced, updated." Randi pointed to a far wall. "I gave them a promo shot from *Wondermancer High* and they moved it next to Gabby and Dash's."

"Ah." Enough said about that. Derek refused to watch the show — well, he was not the target audience for it — because he never believed Randi had a place in television. Not that he thought she was a lousy actress or director, but it kept her from the guitar and the stage, where she belonged. *Let other rock stars pull double duty as actors.*

The waiter arrived with their food and Derek turned his plastic basket to place his onion rings within snatching distance. Randi used to love sampling from his lunches, and it had baffled Derek during subsequent dates here that Randi ordered her usual rather than what Derek ate, since she obviously preferred it. Today, it was the same thing she got every time they'd met. Reuben light on the sauerkraut, and fries.

She kept her hands to herself as well. Derek's onion rings sat there untouched while he worked on his grilled cheese and tomato sandwich. His heart sank a bit.

"Why are we here, Derek?" she asked, wiping off a drop of sauce from her lip.

"We're having lunch. I'm treating you for your birthday."

"You're supposed to treat a woman to steak and lobster on her birthday."

"What if she's vegan?"

Randi held up her sandwich, which was thick with corned beef.

"Shall we say seven tonight?"

Randi chewed, glaring at him.

"Fine." The melted cheddar seemed to lodge in his throat and he tossed back the rest of his soda, then signaled for another one. "I'm promoting a nostalgia tour, all female acts from the eighties."

"Kristy told me about it the other night. When I got your flowers and invite I had a feeling that was the reason you wanted to talk."

She scowled and ate, quite a feat considering Jerry's sandwiches were too amazing for diners to remain grumpy while eating. *Who knew she had the ability to hold a grudge with her appetite?*

"You're going to ask me to join the lineup," she said, not asking. "You want me to support Kathy Kush."

"Actually, I planned it the other way around." When Randi stopped eating he tried to read the expression on her face. She went slack for a moment, as though a bite had slid down the wrong pipe.

After a second, she inhaled and shook her head. "I don't get it. I haven't performed in fifteen years, and it's been twenty since I cut a record. Kathy never stopped, and she released an album this year."

"True, but it's the one old hit keeping her afloat. You know how radio is these days. You've had more songs chart in your career, and with *Wondermancer High* and *Danse Macabre* you have a new generation of fans who've never seen you live," he said. He reached for a crisp, fried ring and willed her to help herself to his food. Not so much a glance at his lunch. It mattered to him, for the sake of memory and normalcy. To his ears, he sounded as though he was schmoozing a stranger and he longed to stand on familiar ground with Randi again.

He dipped a narrow curve of onion ring into the puddle of ketchup on his wax paper lining. *You know you want it, love.* No dice. Defeated, he took a bite.

"Kristy said three acts. Who else is lined up besides Kathy?" Her words promised no commitment from her.

"I'm talking with a few people. I was considering either Denise or booking The Shimmer Sisters." The latter act, a quartet comprised of women who weren't related, had been more of a pop act in their heyday, and none played instruments. Lighter fare than what Randi sang, and Derek caught her displeased reaction.

"Rather a mismatched roster, you think? Kathy's fanbase is nowhere close to the Shimmers', and I don't believe anyone from the original lineup tours anymore. It's like one of the old singer's nieces and her friends." Randi slurped up the rest of her egg cream and pushed aside the glass. "What kind of gong show are you running?"

"One that's in trouble, love." Time to play the desperation card. He'd held out long enough. "You want me to beg you, is that it? Admit that resigning as your manager was the worst mistake of my life and how only you can right this bloody Titanic?"

Randi picked up a limp French fry and dropped it back in the basket. "Why go through with it? I like Kathy, but who's going to pay to see a half-assed Ladies of the Eighties tour when the opening act wasn't even born in that decade? Cancel now and cut your losses."

"It's just not the concerts. I have deals in place for live albums and a documentary crew to follow the bands and create a limited series."

"Yeah? Who agreed to that hot mess?"

"ExStream."

Randi's gut roiled. She wanted a second egg cream, this time with vodka, to fortify her after Derek answered her next few questions.

"So your company is producing this series?" She hadn't followed all the activities involving Derek and the firm he'd inherited from his father. On occasion she'd run into a boy band singer at an event who talked in passing of being managed by one of Derek's junior staff. They'd expanded their stable to include actors and writers, so a jump to production sounded plausible.

Yet, Randi doubted it in this case.

He paused, his shoulders heaving in a quiet sigh. He twined his fingers and set them on the table. Here came the big reveal.

"No. It's being done by, uh, Too True Productions."

Big shock there. Randi turned with a slow burn toward the booths behind her and shot daggers of ice at the two younger women staring back, all doe-eyed and apologetic.

"You wanna fill me in on the latest happenings at work?" she called out. After the most awkward moment of silence endured in her life, she added, "You got something to say?"

Gabby held up one finger, grabbing the waiter's attention. "Yes. We'll take the rest of our sandwiches to go." Then she scooted hard into Jessie and the two stumbled out of the booth, baskets in hand.

"Hey!" Randi stayed put, torn between storming to the front and remaining in place to give Derek what for. "Get back here."

"Sorry, got a meeting in a bit," Gabby said as she slid to the front register to pay. "We love you, Randi!"

Unreal. Gabby knew the whole damn story—the drama, the lost opportunities and Randi's desire to punch Derek in the back of the head. What would possess Gabby to take on a project with him, to say nothing of roping her into a commitment she wasn't sure she wanted?

"For what it's worth"—Derek's voice drew her attention back to him—"I negotiated with Lena DeVito." He nodded toward the front. "I have yet to be formally introduced to Gabby Randall, though it would appear she's been apprised of the deal."

"I'd arrange a meet and greet if she wasn't trying to sneak out with the office manager. I'm surprised Lena's working with you on a documentary show for a tour that's going to cut into *Danse*'s shooting schedule." As Derek opened his mouth she added, "I mean, you want to go out in the spring, yes? We're on hiatus now, and that's when we all meet to start the second season."

"You're on hiatus, yet you have to be back at the office?" He raised an eyebrow.

"A lot of planning goes into a TV series, and its spinoff. But I can't talk about that right now, and neither can you."

"I'd never betray your confidence, love," he said.

Didn't stop you from taking off when I needed you. She fumed in her seat and he took advantage of the silence.

"Randi, if you say no, there's no tour and no film. I can't fathom a Lady of the Eighties lineup without one of the decade's top acts."

She barked out a laugh. Ten names surfaced in her mind and spilled from her lips. "Sign any of them." She shook her head. "I still remember Duncan swooning over how what's her face was gonna be the biggest name on the planet by dancing in her underwear, and he was right."

"Just Duncan." Derek sighed, offering a sad smile. "I miss him."

"Me too. So call *her*."

"I can't afford her."

Randi frowned. "So now I'm cheap."

"It's not a fair comparison. Randi Raucous was metal and hard rock, not Top 40. That's a niche audience, and you kept them in the palm of your hand." Derek ticked familiar names on his fingers and added, "They're either retired from the business or pledged to open for other acts in the coming year. Denise's music crossed over well enough that having her open makes sense."

"You know whose music makes the most sense, if you're looking for hard rock?" Randi peeled away a strip of corned beef and ate it. "Snake Pit."

"Were they an all-female group, and still together, yes." Derek nodded. "Even if I altered this tour to include male acts, Zane can't sing anymore."

"Kristy can."

Derek's eyebrows lifted again, curious.

"You're forgetting Zane produced a single for her in the late eighties."

He snorted. "Yes, a novelty. If I remember correctly, he got the deal for her in hopes that she'd marry him."

"She'd have married Zane if a klieg light fell on him and melted his face. The point is, the song charted so she counts as an eighties lady. Plus, she and Zane had that duet for his first solo album. There's no reason why they can't open with a Snake Pit set with her performing the songs."

She watched for Derek's reaction, to sense if he thought her facetious. In truth, she'd concede to a tour if it meant having the time to spend with one of her closest friends. Kristy loved to sing, and while those around her put little faith in a career for her, Randi never forgot how her friend's face glowed at the idea of performing. Zane had allowed her into the world, with limitations, and when the children had come Kristy's priorities had shifted. Her son and daughter were grown and out of the house now, though, and Randi felt Kristy deserved a chance to pursue her dream.

"Kristy won't go for it," Derek said, firm.

"Why don't you ask her instead of assuming it?"

"I had dinner with them recently. She's a happy grandmother, content to watch sunsets on the bay with her husband."

Heh. He was probably listening in on Kristy's birthday call. Randi took out her phone. "How about I ask her?" she challenged.

Derek's hand reached out, as though to stall her, but one glare kept his touch from connecting. He retracted and sank a bit in his seat. "You realize," he said, "a tour with Kristy and Kathy won't draw much without you to headline."

Randi turned to check the door. Gabby and Jessie were gone. Just as well. They'd hear about this soon enough.

Back to Derek, she said, "You know what? Fine. I'll do this tour on two conditions. One, Kristy and Zane have the first slot. Bill them as Snake Pit if you want, or just as themselves. She'll surprise you."

He looked thoughtful for a moment, but nodded. "What else?"

"After the last show is over" — she took in a deep breath — "I never want to see you again."

.

Chapter Five

"Once again, give it up for Randi Raucous!"

The studio audience whistled and clapped, though not with the same enthusiasm as when she'd performed her first number. In her mind, Randi attributed the decline in enthusiasm to a collective exhaustion. It was well after midnight and she was singing live on a popular late-night variety series. *Anybody coming out to see ninety minutes of music and lame comedy skits has to be hanging by a thread at this point,* she decided.

No, the weak applause had nothing to do with her near disastrous first number, where she'd flubbed the first verse of a song she knew backwards and forwards, then missed a cue after guitarist Brad's solo. She held on to that belief, true or not, to get through the next three and a half minutes. It baffled her, because she'd played before crowds and cameras before without nerves threatening to take over. *What makes this so different?*

She knew the answer. Derek. He consumed her thoughts, day and night, to the point of obsession. She'd decided to do something about it.

The lighting in the studio made it difficult to see deep into the crowd, but as she sang she picked out a few faces. Smiles and nods. Fingers snapping to the beat. She was winning them back—a quick glance at her guitarist confirmed this. She appreciated Brad's support, tonight and throughout the tour. He was like an older brother, watching out for her and winking during numbers to lift her spirits.

Behind her, Greg Orville kept the rhythm. Shortly after she'd signed on with Glissen, relations between members of Snake Pit had unraveled. True to his offer made at their first meeting, Greg had defected from the group to join her act. Randi felt some guilt for poaching him, but when Greg played it assuaged all bad feelings. The man was awesome, and a good friend.

She'd taken to the format of this show with ease. It was her third appearance on American television, impressive given her short career, and the first time she'd played live instead of miming to a recorded track. She hated having to do that, but in those instances no studio audience was watching her. The shows tacked on canned applause to bookend her 'performance'.

For this second and final number of the night, or morning, she sang her first top ten hit. The success of her debut, eponymous album had surprised her. Everything Derek had predicted so far had come to pass, too fast for her to process. The album and first single had gone gold, music video shows had put her in high circulation and A-list acts wanted her to support them. To think just last year she'd felt the thrill of seeing Black Alchemy in concert. Now she was their opening act.

Well, for the North American leg of their tour. Her music hadn't made much headway elsewhere, and Derek planned to change that.

Deep in the dark, people stood one by one and soon she won a full-on ovation as the final chord vibrated to a close. Heaving with exhaustion, Randi lifted her guitar and held it high as Brad closed in on one side and Gary, her bassist, the other. They bowed in unison and the lights on the camera facing them dimmed, signaling the commercial break.

Unlike rehearsal, which enjoyed a more leisurely pace, the switch to the next skit happened with ordered speed. A production assistant escorted the band away from the main set while other hands scurried to set up props and wrangle the featured actors and the guest host to their places. Randi had hoped to linger in the wings to watch, and she knew Greg wanted to split and wind down in his hotel room, but they were all hustled to their shared dressing room. Per the agreement, they all needed to be present for the final cast call in another thirty minutes.

"Getting better, kiddo." Greg slapped her shoulder and brushed past her to the small craft table set up just for their consumption. She still hadn't gotten over all the stuff the show had given her, just to sing for one night. She understood how certain rock acts inserted odd requests in their tour riders — monochromatic candies, specific brands of beer, crushed ice as opposed to cubes — but it tickled her to think some poor gofer had had to bend over backward to find her favorite barbecue corn chips or else incur her wrath.

"I don't care about snacks," she'd told Derek over the phone while packing. "Whatever they have is fine."

"Love, you have so much to learn about being a rock star," he'd said, chuckling.

Randi settled into a comfy chair and draped her legs over the thick arms. Brad and Gary tucked into the sandwiches while Greg reached for the twelve-year-old scotch and crystal glass reserved only for him. He'd earned it.

"You think we can get a TV in here?" she whined. "Came all the way to New York to be on this show. I'd like to see some of it."

"Why? Ninety percent of it sucks." Brad talked with his mouth full of ham and rye. "Hasn't been the same since the original cast cycled out."

"Still..." She was part of an institution now, this long-running variety program, and she felt as if she'd been committed to an institution. She loved the concert life, but it stifled her at times. When she wasn't on stage, people confined her to rooms and buses with little to no freedom. This gig gave her a few days' break from the tour, but she'd seen nothing of the city.

Even if Derek conceded to allowing her a few hours of leave, what then? *How does a person pick one thing to do in New York City?* Right now, she'd as soon choose to sleep.

Her band coaxed her to eat. She wasn't hungry. They debated the merits of the current cast versus the classic players, but she wanted no part of the discussion. If watching the show wasn't possible, she preferred to close her eyes and think of Derek. He'd been scarce for much of the long day and night. Greg had said something about phone conferences with his father, or other people. Forever working, making deals and greasing palms. She never questioned his activities, because whatever he accomplished with a receiver stuck to his ear tended to benefit her.

Still…the idea of Derek with free time, a moment to sit with her and talk, appealed to her. Dare she call it love, what she felt for him? Infatuation, perhaps, or a belated schoolgirl crush. Her eighteenth birthday had passed on the road, with her bandmates splitting a cake that read *Happy 27* in red icing. She crossed her fingers with the hand not holding the fork as she ate.

So she was legal now, and Derek even closer to thirty. Where was the harm in gauging his interest in a romantic relationship? It wasn't as if he'd been a teacher, and she was done with school. The world believed Randi Raucous was in her mid-twenties, anyway, and if she thought about it, Ms. Raucous was more of an extension of Randi Marsh. The woman within her.

It all made her head hurt. Randi looked with longing at the craft table and figured she should have a bite to prevent herself from getting sick. She launched from the chair and nibbled on a few cheese cubes when the sound of quarrelsome voices increased in volume on the other side of the door.

"We didn't rehearse for it," said a woman Randi didn't recognize.

"They're professionals, and equipped to deal with this sort of thing. What other choice do you have?" That was Derek, and when the door opened to admit him and the production assistant, he continued the conversation. "You have a skit on reserve for when this happens?"

"That's the problem. This never happens." The woman talking with Derek wore a headset with a microphone and clutched a clipboard to her chest. "We do, however, have several cast members with backgrounds in improv and enough confidence to fill in the time."

"Five minutes is longer than you realize. It can be an eternity on the telly, love."

"Oh, you are not telling me and my cast how to do our jobs," the woman challenged.

Derek wasn't hearing her. He turned to Randi and the band as though seeing them for the first time. "Get your instruments," he ordered. "You're going back on."

"Sir," the woman protested, "that's not your decision. It's up to Larry—"

Derek whipped back to face her. The clipboard slid a few inches higher to cover the woman's chin. Her only armor.

"I don't suspect Larry will mind, after I speak with him." He winked. Done deal. Final word. Back to Randi, he said, "Well, come on then."

"What?" Randi coughed up a bite of cheddar and covered her mouth to stop it from flying across the room. "What's going on?"

"Eddie was taken away by ambulance." Derek referred to the show's most popular player. Eddie got the most screen time and appeared destined to make the crossover to film. He was scheduled to star in the final skit.

"Is he okay?" Greg asked, and set down his drink.

"Appendicitis, they're saying. They found him passed out in his dressing room." Derek moved deeper into the room toward Randi, his face expressing a mix of concern and excitement. Randi thought of poor Eddie, whom she'd adored at their first meeting, and sent up a quick prayer for his recovery.

"He'll be fine, love, but the show's a few minutes short. It's enough time for one more song." He touched Randi's shoulders to assure her of her ability to save the day, and she tried to ignore how his proximity caused her skin to tingle.

"Doesn't Eddie have a stand-in to perform the skit?" She gave little consideration to the words coming out of her mouth, and Derek showed his obvious displeasure at her reaction. He saw this as an opportunity to boost her career, while she seemed to want to worm her way out of it. She wanted to shrink away, knowing she'd come off as a stubborn child.

"Eddie was doing one of his signature characters. You remember, Randi, we watched the rehearsal." This from Brad, who now stood next to her. "You can't put in a sub for something like that."

"He's right, love. They're going to another commercial soon and they have nothing but dead air ahead unless you get back out there," Derek said. He clasped his hands. "I'm thinking 'Good Vibrations.' It's going to be your next single, so it's the perfect time to debut a telly performance of it."

Randi considered the change in plans. They'd rehearsed the two numbers and nothing else for the show. She'd recorded a sped-up, metal version of the Beach Boys song, with the lyrics tweaked so she sang about a boy giving her the 'excitations', for the album, but had yet to include it on her setlist for the tour. Derek had insisted on at least one cover, and this choice had baffled her, but she'd kept her mouth shut for the sake of keeping peace in the studio.

Making some old tune by a surfing pop band her next single, though...why? If it went gold somebody else would earn money from it. Why not release one of her songs first? She wanted to be recognized for her music.

"Does it have to be that one?" she asked. "The crowd liked our last number. I'd think they want something new—"

"Love." Derek laid a hand on her shoulder, squeezing hard. His eyes darkened a shade and Randi shivered with sudden discomfort. Her manager's attitude cooled with obvious disfavor. "I do the thinking for this outfit. Your job is to play your guitar and sing."

Done deal. Final word.

Seconds of silence passed, and the room lightened again when Derek's smile softened his face. It was as though his personality shifted back to good cop.

"Right. No time to waste, all of you. I'll be with Larry in the booth." He dashed out of the dressing room, leaving an astonished production assistant to follow, slack-jawed and shaking her head.

Greg set down his bottle with a sigh and reached for the drumsticks on the coffee table. "Okay, you heard the man." The rest of the band grunted their displeasure at losing their downtime and lumbered toward the door. Randi remained in place, lost in thought until Greg put his arm around her. "You all right doing this? Derek can be an ass, but if you're not up to another number I'll tell him."

"I'm up for it. I'm a professional, like he said. I have to get used to last-minute changes, right?"

"Maybe, but when you're big time you have the option of saying no," Greg said.

"Am I big time?"

Smiling, he shook his head.

"That's what I thought." She grabbed her guitar and they caught up with the rest of the group. They tuned their instruments as activity flurried around them, and Randi leaned over to Brad. "I wish we were singing something else," she said. "I don't care much for 'Good Vibrations'."

"Not a Beach Boys fan, then?"

"I don't mean that. I like the song, but not the way I recorded it. I'd just as soon perform it the way they did." She sighed. "More than that, I want to do a song I wrote for once."

"Like 'Play It Safe'?" Brad made a face, and she laughed. Yeah, the execs had passed on that one for the first album. Randi still needed to work on it, but she'd grown as a songwriter in this short time.

"I was thinking of 'Do It Again'. I like how that one turned out." It had taken a few weeks to perfect the lyrics and music, with help from Brad. It was a mature love song with an edgy beat, a surefire power ballad hit if somebody higher up gave it a chance. Plus, it shared its title with another Beach Boys song. Maybe Derek wouldn't notice if she made a switch.

Or maybe she'd find another singer in her place when she boarded the tour bus later in the morning.

A different production assistant approached to usher Randi and Brad to their marks. Greg was seated at the drums and Gary noodled on his bass, getting ready. "We're back in thirty," he said. "Mary will introduce you and you go straight into your song."

Randi nodded her understanding and checked her guitar for sound. Before them, the energy radiating from the studio audience crackled and prickled her skin. From what she understood, anybody coming to see the show got what they saw, and skit lists were never leaked to the audience. This time, though, crew had called to set up for Eddie's performance and had been forced to change midstream.

She stood here now, about to put on a show for a crowd who had no idea what to expect. Excited murmurings told her they were pumped for it. For her.

With seconds before go time, she signaled to the band. "Change of plans," she said, her voice a hiss. "We're doing 'Do It Again.'"

"Are you high?" Greg protested. Gary and Brad responded with approval, however, and gave her the thumbs-up. Greg shook his head.

"In five, four..." called out a voice.

Greg got in one final barb. "He's gonna kill you."

"Three..."

"I don't care," Randi said. "This is my career. The Beach Boys have theirs."

Done deal. Final word...until the first lyrics of Randi's song filled the studio.

"What is that? What's she doing?"

This sounded nothing like *Good Vibrations*.

Derek sat in the booth next to Larry, the show's creator, powerless to do anything but watch as Randi disobeyed his direct order. Part of it, anyway. This past week he'd assured Glissen he'd find an opportunity for Randi to perform the cover song ahead of the single's release in order to generate interest. Timing mattered in this business, and the record execs had reasons for asking Derek to exclude the song from her tour set.

The first live performance of *Good Vibrations* by Randi Raucous had to occur under special circumstances, a stars-aligning moment. When the comedian Eddie had been taken away by ambulance, Derek had fought every fiber of his being to tamp down his glee when the extra spot opened for the band.

Instead of wowing eleven million at-home viewers with a hard-grinding metal version of an American pop classic, she was singing…this? It took a few seconds, but he recognized the lyrics of the angsty, lovelorn ballad Randi had pitched to him for possible inclusion on her next album. She'd envisioned it as a signature power ballad—every big act had one—where her song implores her unseen lover to wait for her return from touring so they can engage in what the title implies.

A good writing effort on her part, but the song wasn't ready for the public. The folks at Glissen liked it, but wanted to wait so Randi would have a strong sophomore effort. Derek cringed, thinking about the angry phone messages that no doubt waited for him at the hotel.

Larry leaned in to him, grinning. He smelled of weed and the peppermint that failed to mask it. "Not bad. Where were you hiding this song?"

"Not deep enough," Derek muttered. "Larry, I apologize. This was not the song we agreed on performing. I'm about to thrash her for defying me."

"Can it wait until after the cast call?" Larry pointed to a monitor. "Look at that. They're hanging on every word."

The screen showed the audience, and if one could judge by their reactions Randi had charmed them once again. They nodded in time to her lyrics and thrilled at Brad's dramatic solo. At the song's end, everybody in the bleachers took their feet in unison and the studio shook with their ovation.

The show's director gave the order to keep the band in place. The cast and guest host assembled around them during the station break to prepare for the final curtain call. Feeling useless, Derek left the booth without acknowledging Larry.

He ran into Mary, one of the repertory players, as she dashed toward the set. "Derek, you must be so proud. Randi was awesome!" Her high-pitched voice gushed.

Derek regarded the bubbly, dark-haired beauty with a smile. "She is definitely full of surprises." Not a lie, and if he had to admit it, Randi had turned in a top performance for this last number. If anybody had failed tonight, it was him for not reinforcing the importance of following directions.

Mary sidled closer, her eyes flashing with energy and desire. "You coming to the after-party? It's not far."

"Tempting, but I've a full day tomorrow and I'd hoped to get to bed." At her blatant disappointment, he added, "If that doesn't do the trick I might try sleeping."

The woman winked.

She expected way worse than she got. She expected…emotion. Shouting, anger, at least a silent boiling expression reddening his face before he asked to speak with her in private. Derek said nothing to her after the band had gone rogue on live television. They stood to one side during the last call and absorbed the cheers from crew and audience, took their bows and drifted to the dressing rooms to collect their things. All the while, she waited for a reprimand that never came.

Brad and Gary elected to attend the after-party, but the impromptu performance had drained her. She begged off and followed Greg back to the hotel. They had a late wake-up call, but had to report at noon to board the bus for their next gig in Connecticut. It was close to two and she should be exhausted, but anticipating a showdown with Derek left her wired and anxious.

Greg drew her into a half-hug outside her room. "If it makes you feel any better, Snake Pit pulled much worse shit under his supervision. You haven't ruined your career. He'll get over this."

She wished for her friend's confidence. "Why am I still feeling guilty?"

"It was one song. Glissen can release 'Good Vibrations' regardless of what you sing," he said. "If 'Do It Again' gets recorded and made into a single, all the better. If not, it's out there anyway and you're no poorer for it. It's not like a groupie ODed on the bus under your watch."

Whoa. "That happened to you?"

Greg said nothing else except good night and loped across the hallway to his room. Randi jammed her key into the doorknob and disengaged the lock. She glanced to her left, past the lighted sconce to the next room, where Derek was staying. What was he thinking now? Did he plan to fire her, or send her home? Did he have the authority to do that? Glissen had signed her for three albums, and if anything, the execs ought to be happy to know she had brought down the house tonight. More PR for them.

She knew she wouldn't sleep for a second if she let her anxiety eat away at her brain. She felt no guilt for switching the song—in her heart, the original song served to bolster her career more than a cover. She appreciated everything Derek managed for her, and though she was still new on the scene she wanted to be part of the decision process. Control.

She left the key in the lock, the diamond-shaped tag swinging and tapping against the door. The sound of the security chain zipping free followed her second knock next door and Derek opened it a crack.

He looked bleary-eyed at her, not angry yet not quite pleased. "Randi, love, it's two in the morning. Get some rest."

Randi's heart throbbed wide and hard in her chest. Derek wasn't wearing a shirt, and the sliver of bare chest visible through the crack represented the largest amount of his skin she'd seen. More than once she'd imagined what he might look like without clothes, and here she realized her fantasies had missed the mark. Derek's pecs were covered in tight, wiry curls, about a shade darker than the hair on his head. Her gaze panned down in embarrassment and noticed his right leg was also free of clothing, all the way up his hip.

Holy crap, he's naked.

"I-I didn't mean to cause trouble," she got out, and looked for another point of focus to keep from stammering. "I just wanted to share a song I wrote. I mean, I only have a few on the album and I don't want to be known for doing covers—"

"Randi." Derek shot his head through the opening to silence her. "Let's talk in the morning. The show was exhausting for all of us, so let's let clearer heads prevail over breakfast. Sound good?"

Well, at least she wasn't fired, or being sent back to San Bernardino. She opened her mouth to agree when another voice called from behind the door.

"Derek, honey, who is it?"

Bile bubbled up Randi's throat and she swallowed back. She recognized Mary, the shrill comedienne who performed Valley Girl-style characters and mediocre celebrity impressions. If Derek was naked, no doubt...

Oh hell. "I'm disturbing you," she said. "Sorry about that." She stepped back to retreat to her room, but her mouth acted independent of her brain. "Really? Her?"

"Excuse me." Derek arched an eyebrow. "My private life is not your concern, Ms. Marsh."

Nice, we've reached the cold, formal address part of awkwardness. "You don't seem to have a problem commenting on mine," she shot back.

"That's because I'm responsible for you. You're worth a lot to many people, and it won't do to find you in an alley high or stoned or frothing at the mouth from a bad trip, or murdered."

He sounded like a guidance counselor on a field trip. "Hey, I can take care of myself. I'm not that much younger than you." Not a good time to give away her true age.

"Of course you're not."

Randi didn't miss the change in his tone, from authoritative to skeptical. Had he figured it out? No. Derek was a straight-up guy and he'd have outed her if he knew she was just eighteen.

"You don't think I'm capable of handling myself in sticky situations?" she challenged. Let naked Mary wait. She wanted this done now — more control of her career in all aspects, not just songs. She'd missed out on many side-trip opportunities during the tour because Derek reigned her in at every chance. Meanwhile, Brad and Gary and Greg did whatever the hell they wanted.

They'd travel to Canada soon, her first time in a different country, and she wanted to see more of it besides the interiors of concert halls.

"I don't doubt it, love. In fact, it worries me what you're capable of. Maybe you ought to have more freedom, but…"

She broke in, "Damn straight, Derek. I want what's fair to me." She thought of him, standing naked in his shadowed room, and it saddened her that she wasn't the woman waiting for him to come back to bed.

I'm not afraid to get what I want, either.

Before another thought formed in her head, one that might have called her down from the ledge, Randi lunged forward and grabbed Derek's face. She pulled him close, ignoring how his eyes widened in surprise, and planted a kiss on his lips. The force with which she took charge caused him to lose his grip on the door and he stumbled a bit, almost over the threshold, and exposed himself to the hallway.

Randi moved her lips over his, urging them to let her breach. She willed his arms to encircle her, draw her into a warm embrace and temper her thudding heart. Derek remained frozen.

She tapered off, her gaze cast down to see him, all of him. She gasped. She'd seen naked men before, but *damn*.

"Derek?" Mary called again from the depths of the darkened room. Randi stepped back, heated with embarrassment and a touch of relief. She'd made the move, let him know how she felt, so whatever happened next on tour she could concentrate on work at least.

Derek turned for a second, then regarded Randi again.

"I hope you get everything you want, Randi. Good night." He closed the door and she heard the chain rattle.

"What the hell does that mean?" she asked herself. *I kissed you, say something about it!* Was she in trouble with Derek, or the label? How could she go to sleep with so many questions gone unanswered?

"Dunno. You tell me."

Randi yelped and turned around to see a laughing Brad, half-empty bourbon bottle in hand, hovering close. Her confrontation with Derek must have been intense, because now her bandmate's stench hit her nostrils and she winced.

"Dude, take a shower." She pinched her nose.

"In a sec. You all right?"

Despite the stink of sweat and cigarette smoke filling the air between them, she let Brad drape his arm around her shoulders. They walked in step back to her room, where she ripped the key from its lock.

"I kind of expected Derek to blow up at me, but he didn't. I guess he was too busy thinking about getting laid," she said. *With somebody else.*

"Good for him. He's kind of uptight. He could use it."

Randi shook her head. Of course the men stuck together. She reached for the bottle but Brad jerked it away. "Nuh uh. You're too young."

"I'm twenty-seven."

"Bullshit," Brad slurred, and Randi guessed he held the remaining bourbon in his liver. "Nobody's buying that, except maybe the fans. It's obvious you just turned legal."

Randi said nothing. Her body went cold and she took in a shuddering breath. *Brad knows? What about Derek?* It would explain his aloof behavior after the kiss. He looked out for her not because she was vital to the label, but he still saw her as a child.

Why play along with her lie, though?

Brad's expression slackened and his eyes widened. "Oh, crap. I wasn't s'posed to say that."

"It's fine, dude. Whatever. Here." She guided him to the spare bed rather than the shower. In this condition he might drown under the spray. "Get some sleep." She'd crank up the AC and sleep facing away from him to avoid the smell.

Brad conked out the second his face met the mattress. For his own safety, Randi rolled him all the way onto his stomach and pried the bottle from his fingers. She showered and dressed in clean sweats, then settled in for sleep. Lights from Times Square filtered in through the thin curtains and she focused on one set of blinking lights spelling out a sports shoe logo until the sandman claimed her.

To her mind, mere minutes had passed when a sober, sweeter-smelling Brad was shaking her awake. She rolled onto her back to see him dressed in jeans and a sleeveless tee.

"Randi, girl, what happened last night?"

Everything, nothing. "Huh? What do you mean?"

Brad held up a folded letter on hotel stationery. "Greg said Derek slid these under all our doors. I went back to use my shower, and I found one, too."

Randi took the letter and read Derek's sharp handwriting, announcing to each member of the band his resignation as Randi's manager and the pending arrival of another man in the firm's New York office to replace him.

"Where's Derek now?" she croaked, her voice dry from sleep.

Brad shrugged. "Who knows? He checked out at the ass crack of dawn."

She read Derek's note again. *I hope you get everything you want, Randi,* he'd told her.

"Not this," she whispered. "I don't want this."

Chapter Six

Present Day

"Before we get started, let's have a quick rundown of the rules."

Dash cupped his hands to his mouth. "It's rock and roll! There are no rules!" A multitude of horned finger signs shot upward, and jeers erupted from the small gathering in Randi's garage. Earlier in the day, the actor had helped her clear the space to create a practice area for the band. Friends and neighbors now lined the perimeter, sitting on folding chairs and sturdy crates.

As Randi negotiated her spot on the tour with Derek, she'd insisted her original bandmates got right of first refusal to join her, and of the three, Greg was the sole holdout. She'd expected that, but had to make the offer to her good friend. Now married with a child, Greg had chosen to live out blissful retirement in Montecito, tending to his garden and teaching young Gwen to ride a bike.

Brad and Gary, many years older and grayer on top, still possessed the talent that had helped her sell records in her prime. Brad's son, Junior, rounded out the quartet on drums. Every time Randi glanced in his direction she swore she was looking through a rip in the time-space continuum.

"Says you. Randi owns the house, Randi pays the bills. Unless you want to contribute financially, you'll all be dears and use the trash bins." She pointed to the large rubber cans on either side of the opened garage entryway. "Most important, though, is the second rule — no cameras or recording devices."

A collective groan brought down the mood as phones returned to pockets and purses. "Hey, hey," Randi added, "I may have sold my soul to rock and roll, but my ass belongs to Too True Productions. Recording rights to all performances related to this tour are theirs, so if you have problems you can take it up with those two ladies over there." She pointed to Lena and Gabby, who perched in one corner with their men.

"Nice, way to shift the blame," Gabby said, teasing.

"But we are filming this for the docuseries," Lena piped in, and held up a sheaf of papers. "So we need these release forms signed before the camera starts rolling."

Randi was grateful for the time bought by the legalities involved in making the show. Her stomach churned and she gripped the neck of her guitar to keep her fingers from trembling. Never mind she'd played at least one song every day since mastering the instrument, the gravity of the moment hit her and rattled her nerves. Jamming with friends, sure, she could do it all night. Here she was preparing to go out on the road. Like a professional musician.

She refused to call herself such these days, not since her last album had tanked. When the acting jobs had fallen into her lap, and later *Danse Macabre*, she'd changed her self-perspective. Randi Racuous had gone to pasture years ago, and actress-director Randi Marsh had to find her and drag her sorry butt back into the limelight.

"Okay, class, are all the permissions slips signed and turned in?" she chided the restless crowd. "Good, let's rock." Randi checked the sound of her speaker while her bandmates tested their respective instruments, ready to launch into the first song of the tour's setlist. She listened for the drummer's countdown, her nerves on edge.

Please, Lord, help me pull this off.

* * * *

He was going to kill her.

No. Derek changed his mind. First, he'd yank her by the hair and have her over his lap. Paddle her like a misbehaved child until her bum burned bright red. Then he'd make her sit in a corner, aching from the punishment, then he'd kill her.

Bugger all. The thought of kinky discipline aroused him. He cranked up the AC in his car and let the fans blast. He needed to cool down so he didn't walk into Randi's house with a raging erection.

He'd show, make no mistake. Randi had thought herself clever enough to fudge the time of her first rehearsal on purpose so he'd miss it, but she apparently hadn't counted on Lena DeVito. He'd been having dinner out when he'd checked his social phone app and seen the picture of Randi tuning up in her garage on Lena's feed.

I get to preview the Randi Raucous Band before they go on tour. Jealous? #RAWK

At her age, Randi kept up the high school shenanigans. He'd hoped for her to have gotten all that out of her system. It shouldn't have surprised him, all those years ago, when she'd pulled that stunt on live television. Why connive him now into missing this rehearsal party?

She was still mad at him. She also wasn't the only one guilty of childish, petty acts. He thought back to that night and her little victory with the studio audience. If he closed his eyes he'd see the crestfallen expression of a young, impressionable woman discovering him with a one-night stand. That was when he'd realized Randi might want more from her relationship with him than professional guidance.

Well, that and the kiss. *What a stunner.* Randi had kept that card close to her chest.

And what did he do? Slink away in the middle of the night, much like Mary Whatsherface had after he passed out post-orgasm.

Water under the bridge now. Fodder for some tell-all memoir. At least Mary had complimented him on his sexual prowess, so he'd heard.

He'd gotten the check and had his leftovers boxed, and now he was crawling his car up a side street in Randi's neighborhood for a place to park. Everybody invited to this gig drove alone, it seemed. Cars lined curbs and clustered in the small cul-de-sac by her back gate. He ended up a few well-lighted blocks away, and when he arrived he paused to listen. Her voice rang out clear and bold, performing one of her earlier hits.

It was like stepping through a time machine in this moment. His heart swelled, remembering her audition for Glissen, then her first sound check before opening for Idle and Wild. "You still have it, love," he said.

A fragrant, familiar aroma took his attention from the music, and he heard a cough. Turning, Derek noticed a small group huddled by a large potted plant against the adobe wall separating Randi's home from a neighbor. They talked and giggled and one of them glanced his way and offered a sloping grin. The man's face was mottled by shadow.

"She on 'Do It Again' yet?" he called to Derek.

This person didn't look old enough to have heard the song during its first run. "This is 'Play It Safe'." He pointed toward the garage.

A second man snickered and swayed, long gone with the weed. "Dude, she ain't ever doing that song live again. She said so."

"That's stupid, it's her biggest song. That's like Pharrell having a concert and not singing 'Happy.'" The first speaker glared at Derek as if to say, *Am I right?*

Derek shrugged. They were missing a good show and so was he. He tested the pedestrian gate and, on not seeing a guard, slipped through to the back driveway. People had spilled from the garage, which was strung up with twinkle lights along the edges, and danced and sang with Randi. His gaze settled on Randi, casual and cool in a loose T-shirt and jeans, as she danced her fingers across the neck of her black guitar. Not a red one like she'd played at the height of her career—Derek made a note to procure one for her. He wanted everything involved with her act as authentic as possible to keep with the tour's theme. Same stage setups, lighting and design, and attire if Randi consented.

She could do her hair any way she wished.

Play It Safe ended with its signature flourish and the band took their bows. She'd had a rough time with that song, but after several drafts and tweaks to the melody it had gone on to become one of her greatest hits. Derek guessed the song would serve as the finale of her set, which meant the encore song was next.

Come on, love. He wanted her to prove those stoners in the cul-de-sac wrong. *Play it.*

Instead, Randi lifted the guitar and stepped out of the confines of the neck strap. The celebratory vibe present in her driveway and backyard seemed to dull with the collective realization of the concert's end. No encore. No *Do It Again*. Denied.

"Thank you, everybody," Randi called out to the crowd. "I needed your energy tonight, but I am beat. That's the most I've sang in one night in, like, forever." This earned her some understanding and the applause crested high again. "Folks, I hate to be a bad hostess but I gotta take a break. Y'all have a good night."

Derek watched her hug Brad and Gary, then high-five the drummer. Lena came forward and the two women chatted for a moment. He got the impression the producer had been charged with ushering people toward various exits. Randi disappeared into the house while Gabby and Lena and Dash rounded up the guests.

He refused to leave without talking to Randi. This night had happened because of him.

He was almost to the back door when a hand touched down on his shoulder. "Mr. Hynde?"

"Hello, Mr. Gregory."

"You can call me Dash. We're all casual here." The younger man smiled. "I just wanted to thank you for offering Randi this opportunity. I know she wouldn't want it getting out"—he leaned in and lowered his voice—"but I can tell she wants to go back out on the road."

"That's very kind of you say, Dash."

Dash nodded. "Back when we worked on *Wondermancer*, we'd beg her to tell stories about her rock-and-roll days. Much as she liked acting on the show, though, we knew she wanted to be in the studio or something like that."

It's where she belongs. Derek turned all the way around to converse with Dash. It was okay—Randi wasn't going anywhere at present. "I hope it won't be too much of a disturbance in your shooting schedule."

"It's fine. I don't like long breaks anyway, and all the cast and crew want VIP tickets, so there's some incentive." Dash laughed, but the mirth was fleeting. Derek took a step back as though to taper off their talk when Dash said, "Did I mention I'm on guard duty tonight?"

"Come again?"

Dash indicated the door. "You're not going in there. Tonight took a lot out of her. She needs to wind down."

"Dash, I'm the one who set up this tour. It's in my best interest that Randi is rested and focused. You don't think I'm going to rile her up?" *What nerve.* It irritated him to think the *Danse Macabre* people intended to play gatekeepers for the next few months. They weren't to be involved in the concerts at all. "We're on the same team here."

Dash shrugged. "All I know is every time your name is mentioned Randi gets this look in her eyes, and it ain't affection."

"I missed most of the rehearsal, Dash. I just want a few minutes to talk to her. Randi can't dodge me forever."

The younger man sighed and his gaze drifted toward the driveway. People took their time filtering through the gate while Lena directed somebody to collect discarded cups and plates. Dash seemed to look that way for permission, while Derek remained near the door wondering why he needed it.

"I've also known Randi for years, Dash. I know all her cues, and I promise I won't aggravate her."

"This can't wait till morning?" Dash asked.

"When she's refreshed and full of renewed energy to dodge me some more?"

Dash snorted. "If Gabby catches you, I don't know how you got past me. Of course, Randi doesn't need my protection. She kicks ass in her sleep." With a clap on the shoulder to wish him luck, Dash loped away.

Randi's house, like many in the neighborhood, was built in the Spanish colonial style. It was L-shaped, with the sliding door cut halfway and leading to a large kitchen. Derek took in the white adobe walls and red-tiled roof, and the long wooden plant boxes under each window. Alongside the driveway lush vegetation took up half the backyard, and Derek imagined that with her busy schedule Randi hired a landscaping service to keep everything beautiful and inviting.

Inside, the décor kept the theme. Terracotta tiles and brilliant blue countertops gave the kitchen a homey, comfortable atmosphere. He could picture a family gathered around the large butcher block in the middle, enjoying Sunday brunch.

Seeing Randi here, cooking up a multi-course meal, was a challenge. He never figured her for a gourmet, as she had eaten drive-thru of every variety while on tour and had fidgeted in nicer restaurants. Of course, time passed and people changed, and he wanted to know the Randi of now. He studied all the clues going deeper into house.

After a wrong turn toward the laundry room, he found the spacious living area with its muted beige, brown and clay colors. Large, framed paintings of desert landscapes graced the walls. Potted palms at the corners gave the room a hint of color. In the center were two tan suede sofas facing each other, separated by a wooden coffee table laden with pillar candles at various stages of melt.

On the couch closest to the entryway, Randi lay on her back with her arm draped over her eyes. One foot was propped on the arm and the other touched the floor. She breathed steadily, but Derek doubted she slept. He'd seen her in this position before, on buses and in green rooms, playing possum before a show.

"Go away, Derek," she muttered, surprising him.

He leaned to one side for a better look at her. No way she could see him through her arm. "How did you know?"

"I can smell you. Nobody else I know uses that cologne."

"That's because it's no longer produced. I've been using the same bottle for decades." He chuckled. "A little dab goes a long way."

"It must. You always smelled like you showered in musk." Randi lifted her arm and she glowered at him.

"I see you managed to charm Dash. How else would you have gotten in?"

"You lied to me about the rehearsal party, Randi." He tired of the banter. Time to get serious.

"No, I told you it was tonight." Randi reached for her front pocket and pulled out her phone.

"You gave me the wrong time."

She moved as though to confirm the text. "Typo. Also, you didn't RSVP."

"You can admit you'd rather I stay away."

"I thought I had." Randi wrinkled her nose. "Not that it matters. You'll linger."

"Damn it all." Derek stormed forward and surprised her. Randi pulled up into a sitting position, feet on the sofa and knees against her chest, when he sat beside her. "Do you intend to act difficult for the duration of this tour? How many more times must I apologize for events that happened decades ago?" Time hadn't softened hard feelings, to his distress. What more was needed to warm her to him?

"This is a big deal for me, Derek." Her voice sounded small and it wrenched him. Her tough façade rippled for a moment and he saw the vulnerable young woman he'd discovered in a seedy green room. "I haven't performed in public in years. I wanted friends around me this one night, for support."

"Am I not your friend, Randi?" he asked. "You may think it isn't necessary I be present when you sing, but I've always loved watching you perform. At one point in my life I lived for it."

Randi pushed out a noise of disbelief. She was thinking of that night, he surmised.

"Stop it," he ordered, and she raised an eyebrow in surprise. "You want the truth? It wasn't smart disobeying me on live television, but you crushed it. I was angry, yes, but looking back I'd have to say that version of 'Do It Again' was your best."

"Thanks." Randi looked away.

"I can't wait to hear it on tour."

"Don't hold your breath."

"Your fans will expect it," he said.

"My fans are lucky to see me onstage at all, more so if I don't make an ass of myself." Her feet touched the floor and she hugged herself. "We all had a good time tonight, but I've played much better."

He waited, thinking perhaps the reason she'd fudged the rehearsal time had more to do with sparing her the embarrassment of delivering a poor show to her former manager. A backyard full of drunk friends from work were likely to stroke her ego regardless of how she performed, but Derek remained blunt and honest with her.

"I wouldn't have offered this to you if I wasn't certain you were the right one to headline this tour," he said. "If you have doubts, know you also have time. It'll come back."

"What if it —?"

She never completed the question. Any more negative energy threatened to destroy her confidence. Derek had to fix this, do his job.

Randi needed encouragement, but in that moment his own desires caught up to him, and instead of a kind word he leaned over and kissed her.

Thirty years after that first spark of curiosity, that first yearning to feel his lips against hers, it happened. He made the first move.

Worth the wait? She considered the question as Derek pressed closer, drawing her into his arms and prying her mouth to take in more of him.

His cologne no longer irritated her. His body, hard and unyielding as she shifted in her seat, supported her now-melting form.

Worth the wait.

Wait… She was supposed to hate this man's guts. Damn the hormones clouding her good judgement. She tried to twist and taper off this kiss but one slip of Derek's lip over hers, his tongue probing deeper, kept her rooted.

She warred with herself in that moment — her brain battling her heart and losing — and she scrambled to think of things to get her out of the mood and off the sofa. There was a backyard full of people on the other side of the far wall. How many of them were trampling on plants or whizzing in the bushes? Who was snapping photos of her garage for their social feeds, or helping themselves to the twenty-pound bag of birdseed?

Work. Think about work. Great job, but totally not sexy. She loved the show, and despite directing naked actors to dry hump each other, it seldom turned her on. Randi appreciated the human form, but arousal came in more intimate moments…much like this one.

Derek's hand trailed up her side and cupped her breast. Through the thin layer of cotton, his heat caused her to shudder. He leaned in hard and soon her body slid over the suede, down and back to recline as he covered her.

"Still don't wear a bra, do you, love? Nice," he muttered after breaking the kiss. He brushed his lips over the shell of her right ear, then licked a path to her neck. Randi focused on the ceiling and floated in her body, aware of her movements but feeling as though her limbs acted of their own accord. Like Randi Raucous had taken over.

How does Derek know I never wear a bra?

Add mind-reading to his skillset. His breath seared her skin as he laughed. "Yes, I know a lot of things you thought you hid so well."

She realized he wasn't talking about bras anymore. Of course. He had to have figured out the true gap in their ages by now. Lying with him in her home, in her late forties, didn't hold the same level of forbidden as her old fantasies.

Correction — Randi Raucous, not Randi Marsh. The hard-rockin' teen with the goofy name wanted the older man. The woman currently behaving like a horny teenager wanted...

Derek took her mouth again in a brain-melting kiss. His thigh pried her legs apart and one slow thrust against the crotch of her jeans got her wet.

...wanted this.

Let's try this mind-meld again. Touch me. She moaned when, seconds later, Derek brushed his thumb over her the neck of her tee. It didn't yield, so he moved over one nipple, which hardened and tingled.

All this time, she watched the ceiling and listened. It grew quiet — maybe everybody had left. It worried her, because it meant Gabby could come in at any moment to check on her.

Yep. Any second now. Walk into the room and gasp.

Of course, with Derek's heavy breathing and her racing heartbeat filling her ears, Gabby may have discovered them and tiptoed out the back, no doubt giddy at the thought of Randi getting some after a fair drought.

These jumbled thoughts threatened her arousal, and Randi closed her eyes and gave into the increasing passion. Her shy demeanor baffled her. Her virgin days were so far behind her, her mental rearview mirror no longer reflected their memories. She'd lived the rock-and-roll life in her peak years — men, women, a group or two — and in all those instances she'd never dissected the situations as she was with Derek here in her home.

He reached between them and stroked her between her thighs. That did it. She clutched his bottom and squeezed. His body tensed and pulsed. Promising.

Then he pulled away and groaned, and ruined everything. "I have to go."

"What?"

He left her breathless and dazed and, to her confusion, somewhat relieved. When Derek pushed upward to sit, she noticed his flushed face — still handsome but crestfallen — and felt the air cool.

"I came here originally to give you hell for cutting me out of tonight's rehearsal," he said.

"So you're finishing the job by leaving me on the edge."

"Come again?"

I haven't yet, you asshole. "Nothin'," she muttered.

Derek sat again and took her hand, turned up the wrist and laid a soft kiss. "We have to work together to make this tour a success, Randi. No more sneaking around behind my back. Kristy will be in L.A. soon and it's important we're all in sync."

"I know." In retrospect it had been shitty of her to leave him out of tonight's festivities, but she told herself her reason was valid.

"I'll call soon." He moved to stand but instead leaned close to her. "You're serious about never wanting to see me again after this tour, yes?"

Randi said nothing, but stared him down. He'd always used those kind eyes to his advantage. They were so calm and hypnotic.

"If you mean it, at least give me the favor of making love to you once before it's over." He kissed her again and walked with soft steps back through the kitchen. Her gaze fixed on his exit and blurred a bit when Gabby and Lena emerged, looking his way with twin expressions of confusion.

"Who let him in?" Gabby asked. "I told Dash to watch the back door."

"Derek has his ways," Randi said, getting to her feet. She'd turned to rubber and grasped the sofa for support. A cold shower to wash away the night's sweat and lust sounded awesome right about now. She took one step and wobbled, but before she collapsed Lena charged forward to lend her support.

"Randi, you okay?" The younger woman frowned and cast an angry glance toward the kitchen. "Did Derek hurt you —"

"No, nothing like that. If anything, I brought it on myself."

Gabby and Lena looked at each other, appearing unable to figure that out. Lena asked, "You want to elaborate?"

"I'd rather clean up and go to bed." Not alone, for either of those things. She glanced past her friends to the hallway leading to the kitchen. No shadows moved, no voices drifted her way. Derek was gone for the night, in the physical sense.

He remained in her head, though, all through her goodbyes to Lena and the Gregorys and during her bedtime ritual. When she slipped under her comforter and closed her eyes, his chiding voice sounded louder in her ears.

'Give me the favor…' He wanted her, had just come out with it. Asked to make love to her like inviting her to a formal event.

She'd wanted that so long ago, or rather had fantasized about it. She turned onto her side and thought of how teen virgin Raucous might have reacted had Derek consented to take things beyond a kiss.

What would grown-up Randi do? Moreover, would she want to retract her earlier wish to part ways forever?

Chapter Seven

1986

Randi leaned to her right and whispered in Greg's ear, "My boobs are itching."

"Big deal. So are my balls."

Randi squirmed in her seat, yearning to stick her hand into the vise-tight bodice of her strapless cocktail dress and tug away the underwire shaping the cups, which were a size too small. She'd heard the TV camera added ten pounds, and she imagined every time one zoomed in on her it no doubt looked like her tits were about to explode from this shining sausage casing of an outfit her new management insisted she wear.

Good thing, then, they were sitting in the front row. Less of a chance of knocking somebody in the back of the head with a wayward breast in the event of a ripped seam.

She'd come to this awards ceremony, the biggest one in the music industry, with Greg because neither of her parents were able to accompany her. Mom had fallen ill and Dad felt skittish about leaving her alone. Management had suggested pairing her off with some hotshot actor, but she'd balked. They wanted to create a relationship for the media to cover, and she wasn't interested in fake-playing house with anybody.

She suspected, too, they feared she'd ask a woman to be her date and therefore risk losing her fanbase. Heaven forbid. She figured she'd gain more male fans, assuming they fantasized about their idol involved in some hot girl-on-girl action.

She clutched Greg's hand, thankful he'd agreed to be her date, considering everything that had gone down after she'd split with Derek's company.

Ugh. Perspiration beaded under the swell of her breasts and her butt numbed. To think she used to love watching these awards on TV as a kid. Back then, at least, she'd had the option of moving around or getting a snack. In this life, as a nominee, it was all hurry up and wait while they sat through every single commercial break.

"Why don't you scratch?" she asked. "Nobody's looking."

"Everybody's looking," Greg grumbled and crossed his legs. He'd started a beard since their last meeting and it was growing in nicely. Randi noticed flecks of gray and understood the gap in their ages. She sat here tonight at the beginning of a promising career, while he appeared tired and ready to wind down.

"You've never been nominated, have you?"

"Once," Greg said. "Zilch."

"That sucks."

He shrugged. "I still make money. You know what they say, it's an honor to be nominated."

Ah, yes. A line of bullshit meant to placate sore losers. No different from being runner-up in the senior high talent contest, losing to — of all things — a ventriloquist act. Randi held on to that memory, thinking of Tony DiPesto and wondering if he was watching tonight. She might not win any awards, but at least she'd gone farther in Hollywood than he and his wooden puppet.

As it stood now, she was zero for four with one category left. Every time a presenter announced a competitor's name, though, an odd sense of calm took over. She'd lost the awards for Best New Artist — which was fine, because winners' careers tended to tank after that particular victory — and Female Rock Vocal Performance earlier in the evening. Next came Best Rock Album, which went to a band managed by Derek's group. She cringed when the lead singer thanked Derek, and the large screen on stage showed the agent in the audience, gorgeous in a tux and on the arm of some brunette.

They sat a few rows behind them, on the opposite end of the auditorium. Derek knew she was here — the host had zinged her in his opening monologue and she'd been shown laughing at the joke. Would he try to track her down after the show?

If she left after her last category, she could avoid the possibility. Either way, she wanted out of this dress before she suffocated.

"If I don't win, I'm heading to the little girl's room," she told Greg. "Wanna wait five minutes and meet me in the green room?"

Greg smiled at her. "What if you win?"

"Get real." Her last shot at gold tonight was Best Rock Song, the one category she knew she'd lose. It was awarded to the songwriter, and she'd been nominated for *Do It Again*. She'd recorded an improved version for her new label, which had released it as a single ahead of her sophomore album. When she'd gotten out of her contract with Derek's firm, Glissen had turned one-eighty on her and used a loophole to cancel her record deal. Their perceived loyalty to Derek stung, but at least she was able to record elsewhere.

The song and her second LP had come out in time to be eligible for this year's ceremony, and she was up against songwriting legends, people she worshipped. The thought of being shortlisted for this category gave her extreme imposter syndrome, yet at the same time she basked in the satisfaction of knowing a song Derek hadn't thought was ready for TV was so honored.

On the third hand, she'd written the song about Derek. If she won, she'd have to give him some credit. *What do I root for here?*

She heard a countdown, alerting the audience to the end of the commercial break. Two previous winners from the night, both women Randi had looked up to as a child, came onstage to present her category. The moment passed her in a haze. A clip of *Do It Again* blasted overhead during the reading of the nominees and people applauded. She detected the camera aiming for her, and her face ached with the smile. Seconds later, another singer-songwriter and his partner rose to cheers to accept the award.

Oh for five. Well, crap.

Shite.

Derek gave a slow, soft clap as the winners of Randi's last category ascended the stage. Politics, pure politics had prevented Randi from getting any trophies tonight. She'd come into this award ceremony against tough competition, to be sure, but in the end the honors had gone either to voter favorites or veterans in the industry who hadn't won at the peak of their careers, when they deserved it.

A fine example here, Derek noted. The men who'd beaten Randi for Best Rock Song had decades of classic anthems to their credit, but this win wasn't anywhere near masterpiece level. The academy may as well have slapped a 'lifetime achievement' sticker on the trophy's nameplate.

He sighed and glanced at his companion for the evening. Mavis had worked for JZD Entertainment for five years as a junior manager and arranged a major multi-album deal for one of their clients. Her husband was currently deployed and Derek had figured she needed a fun night out to combat the loneliness. So far it was, though Mavis had somehow turned this into a working 'vacation'.

She excused herself during the next commercial break and came back with two business cards. "Did you know The Plaid Stamps fired their agent?"

More like set him on fire. The punk band had a reputation. "Not interested."

Mavis pouted. "Come on. Yeah, they come off like assholes during interviews, but they're still a draw. They don't have to be a marquee client, but I think we could do well by them."

"Only if they evolve, and act their age. Punk is on the way out, anyway." Derek saw it with similar acts who were morphing into metal or new wave. Tastes were changing, and managing a group like The Plaid Stamps might be palatable if they cooperated. Derek doubted it.

"Well, don't tell him that," Mavis murmured, pointing to a man in leather sitting a few rows ahead of them. Derek recognized him and chuckled.

"I don't have to. He knows the market and he's singing to it."

Mavis sat higher in her seat and glanced toward the front row. "Randi Raucous looks great tonight."

Always has. His heart panged when he thought, for a second, his former client turned their way. Instead of locking gazes, Randi shifted in place to chat up somebody in the row behind hers. Derek and Mavis were a good distance away, but he detected the disappointment and weariness etched on the young woman's face. She'd been shut out this evening and it had to bruise her ego. Somebody not familiar with the business might shrug and say wait till next year, but guarantees didn't exist in such a fickle industry.

"Have you thought about offering to manage her again?"

Mavis' question brought him out of his reverie. He looked his companion in the eye, certain she'd flipped her wig. "Randi would just as soon eat nails."

"It's possible she's amenable to coming back, Derek." Mavis leaned closer and lowered her voice. "I have ears at Gemini. They're not treating her well."

"How's that?" he asked, feeling protective. It had burned him when he'd read the news of Randi's defection to the rival firm. He'd resigned from working with her, but it didn't mean she had to jump ship altogether. JZD employed many competent people ready to grow her career. Too late, he realized how his actions had affected her.

Before Mavis began to explain the music swelled, signaling the return to the ceremony. She settled back to watch the next presenter but Derek kept his eye on Randi as she and Greg left their seats to a pair of fillers and strolled up the aisle toward the exit.

"Where're they going?"

"What did you say?" Mavis whispered in his ear.

He turned his head to acknowledge his companion but, after a second, returned his attention to the far aisle. Randi and Greg weren't taking the exit leading to the green room, where presenters and nominees had access to a craft table and room to smoke. They were leaving altogether.

She might be out of his life for good after passing through that door, and trapped in a bad management deal.

He got to his feet, bending to ease out of the row. "You don't mind if I pop off for a moment?"

Mavis smiled. "Of course not. Go get her."

"Are we headed for the bar, then?"

Randi looped her arm in Greg's and shook her head. "I'm still too young to drink, remember?"

"Nobody's going to card Randi Raucous." Greg laughed.

"Maybe not, but I'd rather drown my sorrows in a Neapolitan shake."

Greg nodded. "Burgers it is."

They pushed through the doors and nodded to the people stationed at the auditorium's entrance, whose sole task tonight was to make sure the doors snicked shut in silence with every exit. People in formal wear — ranging from elegant to neon and mesh couture — milled in the lobby, either taking a break from the ceremony or giving interviews with the few reporters and camera crews allowed in the space. Randi heard her named called and her peripheral vision caught cameras and microphones waving in her direction, but she nudged Greg to keep walking.

She had no desire to give sound bites to stupid questions. *How does it feel to be shut out at the industry's biggest awards? How the fuck do you think? It sucks!*

"Randi, do you have a moment for Music24/7?" a woman shouted.

"No," she barked over her shoulder.

"Is it true you're dating Justin LaPierre?" the reported persisted. "What would he say about you attending this event with another man?"

Justin LaPierre. The closeted actor her management wanted to link to her. *They must have planted a few seeds in the media. The assholes.*

Greg turned back to speak, "Justin LaPierre can lick my itchy—"

She jabbed her friend in the stomach and shouted over him, "I said I don't have time for you guys."

"What about me, love?"

She stopped. Greg skidded to a halt and squeezed her arm. The sudden stiffness of his body mirrored hers as her heart pulsed at a rapid rate. She'd hoped to get out of here without meeting Derek, but fate—like her current management—wanted to dictate events for her.

After a deep breath she turned around and tried not to sigh at the sight of the handsome gentlemen appraising her with soft eyes and full lips curved in a smile. She still remembered the taste of smoke and whisky on them. *Damn his James Bond good looks.*

"You want to go?" Greg's voice rumbled in her ear.

"I'm good." This was inevitable. Better to get an encounter done now than spend the rest of her life asking *what if*. If only several cameramen weren't creeping closer as though sensing a hot story.

"Greg" — Derek nodded at him — "you look well."

"Yeah, for a change." Greg brushed his lips against Randi's hair. "I'll go check on the car." He ignored reporters whispering his name as he walked away.

Derek took a step forward. "You look quite lovely tonight, Randi."

"I look like a party favor at the Playboy Mansion." She couldn't see her hair as she shook her head, but knew not one strand moved. The crew her management had sent to her apartment had all but shellacked her. The sad smile on Derek's face seemed to confirm to her what he thought. Everything she'd fought for with him, and won, she'd failed with this new group. They tarted her up — teased, exploded mullet, slutty outfits, heels that hurt her feet. She looked at Derek and saw pity, and hated it.

She needed to walk away from this conversation with her chin high, and the impression she was better off without his guidance. In truth, she hated the people at Gemini. The only good thing to come out of the relationship was the success of *Do It Again*, but it felt hollow in the wake of the award shutout and the fact nobody from the firm had bothered to show tonight.

"I'm sorry, er…"

She cringed. Oh, he was the last person from whom he wanted sympathy. Not in public, with these vultures pricking up their ears.

"That is to say, I'm sorry so much time has passed since we last spoke," he said. It was a good save. "I owe you an explanation for New York."

"No, you don't. Things happened. It's show business." Like hell would she apologize for anything having to do with that night.

"Fine. Well…" He scratched the back of his neck. "I don't suppose you'd be free one day for coffee, or lunch? I'd like to talk about your contract with Gemini, and the possibility you might be interested in coming back to JZD."

Hooray and hallelujah. Despite the relief flooding her, she fought back a smile. She'd learned much from Greg in the time since leaving Derek's firm. *Don't show your emotions, and listen to every word spoken. Don't let anyone think you're desperate to get out of a bad situation, else they may take advantage and lead you into something worse.*

"I don't know, Derek," she said, keeping her voice low. "The new image aside, I can't complain. My sales are good, and they're looking into ways I can branch out. Film," she added when Derek raised an eyebrow. "They're vetting a few scripts for me."

"You're not an actress, Randi."

Whoa. Where did that come from? The tone in Derek's voice implied she hadn't the skill to become a double or triple threat in show business. "Yeah, I'm aware of that," she said, defensiveness rising as she answered. "In Hollywood, though, they have these things called acting classes—"

"What I mean to say it's not the path I'd choose for you." He shrugged. "I understand a good number of singers go on to vanity film and television projects, but it's a good way to lose focus of the one thing that makes you special."

"So…what? Are you saying I couldn't be special while starring in a movie?" she asked. Several musicians who'd made the crossover to the big screen with great success came to mind. Some had even won awards, and not for writing film scores, but for acting. Despite her irritation with the people at Gemini, they'd assured her of her capability to do the same in a musical built around her.

"Were I still managing your career—"

"But you're not," she broke in. "You made the decision to leave, and I hope you regret it now and every day for the rest of your life, especially when I'm accepting my own little golden man next year."

He frowned. "What...?"

Randi turned sharply in a circle and stormed away, ignoring the bright, tiny explosions of flashbulbs and people calling her name. The scent of Derek's aftershave faded with every step toward the exit and freedom. Along the way her heart grew heavier and doubts increased in volume inside her head. What the hell had she done? Derek had offered her an out, an escape from the bungling manager assigned to her by Gemini, and she'd let her ego take control. Sure, she had no acting chops, but right now Derek's disapproval of something she wanted shattered her desire to leave a bad situation.

This left her with two choices—make the best of her relationship with Gemini, or find a lawyer to get her out of her contract so she might find a better firm to help her. The latter would take time, but man, a movie deal where she got to choose her leading man and write the soundtrack...

Greg was waiting for her by their hired car, and she waved at the onlookers posted on either side of the red-carpeted walkway as they cheered and shouted for her attention.

"How'd it go?" he asked as they ducked into the back seat.

"He offered to bring me back to JZD and I said no."

Greg snorted. "That was dumb."

Randi settled into her seat, forehead pressed against the tinted window. "Yeah."

She'd had enough of glitz and glamour for one night. They gave their directions to the driver, and spent the rest of the evening in their itchy formalwear, signing autographs and drowning sorrows in fast food.

✳ ✳ ✳ ✳

Present Day

Randi eased her bike to a stop just inside the curved drive, behind an SUV bearing a trio of stick figures on the back window. Papa with a straw hat and spade, Mama brandishing a tennis racket, and their little princess cuddling a puppy. It never failed to bring a smile to her face to see it, and the accompanying house evoked similar homey thoughts.

The cottage resembled a smaller-scale TV family home with its split-level structure and stone exterior. Kimberly, Mrs. Orville to the society set, was half her husband's age and missing a sense of humor. She was the gatekeeper here, a true mama bear, but Randi had connections.

"And there she is," she crowed, arms opened wide as Greg's five-year-old girl ran from the front yard to leap into a hug. A huge black Lab galloped close and circled Randi's legs. "Hey, sweetie boo." She planted a loud smacking kiss on Gwen's cheek and cradled the girl in one arm while she patted the scruff of the dog's neck. "Hey there, Pickles."

Gwen held an action figure in her chubby fist. "Did you come to play, Aunt Randi?"

"You know I did, but can I see your daddy first? It's been a long time."

"You never visit just me," Gwen accused. The girl exaggerated, but maybe it seemed that way in her young mind. As godmother, Randi had come to the house often when Gwen had been a toddler, but Kimberly's constant hovering had put her off as if the woman anticipated Randi might whisk the baby onto the back of her motorcycle and head to Tijuana for a wild weekend. Rather than inspire any discord in the Orville household, Randi had scaled back on appearances and sent gifts on holidays and birthdays, and video chatted with the girl when Greg called.

"I'm sorry, sweetie boo. You know Aunt Randi works all the time. They need me in Hollywood to make all those TV shows for grown-ups to watch." She walked up the front yard over a stone path that led to the expansive garden in the back. On a gorgeous day like this, she counted on Greg puttering around instead of lurking in the house. She didn't want to risk the doorbell and have Kimberly answer.

No such luck. Kimberly rounded the corner and skidded to a halt in front of them, her expression pure panic. The young mother sagged and exhaled before reaching out to take Gwen from Randi's arms. "Oh, honey bunny. You know better than to run away like that."

"I heard Aunt Randi's motorcycle."

Kimberly's glare seared Randi. "What if a car came speeding up the road, Gwen? You could've been seriously hurt."

A car. Speeding. Up their front lawn with the huge privacy bushes blocking the house from the road. The Orvilles lived on a cul-de-sac in an upscale community. If anything stood to threaten the peace here, it might be the motorized scooter belonging to the elderly neighbor Randi had met at a barbecue last year.

Say nothing, Randi reminded herself, smiling at Kimberly. *Keep the peace for Greg's sake. Happy wife, happy life.*

"I'm always careful when I pull my bike into the drive," she said.

"I know, Randi. It just worries me when Gwen's not in my sights." Kimberly held her daughter close. *Lord help me if the girl asks for surfing lessons one day.*

"Where's Greg?"

"We were having tea out on the lanai." The tone in Kimberly's voice implied Randi was about to ruin their good time.

"I won't be long, I promise. I need to talk to him about something important."

"Stay for dinner," Gwen said. "Mama's making sp'ghetti."

Randi grinned, then laughed when Pickles landed his front paws on her hip. "Easy, boy. We'll see, sweetie boo. I gotta talk to your daddy first."

To her relief, Kimberly didn't follow her into the backyard. Maybe the idea of hosting Randi for dinner irritated her to the point she wanted to escape to the house, but at this point Randi shrugged off any ill feelings. She found her former bandmate — mentor, surrogate big brother, closest friend outside the *Danse*

Macabre circle—lounging with a book. When he saw her, he attempted to stand but Randi waved him to stop.

She leaned down to kiss him, then moved a downturned paperback on the adjacent lounger to sit. "Retirement becomes you." She said it every time they met, like a ritual.

"I see you made it unscathed."

Randi knew he was talking not about the bike ride, but getting past Kimberly. "Why doesn't she like me? I'm nice to her...you know, in my way."

"She likes you, Randi. It's jealousy."

"What?" Randi straightened in her seat, then hunched over. "She's living the dream. Beautiful house, awesome kid, the best husband ever...why's she jealous of an old lady who works twenty hours a day?"

Greg tilted his head, thinking. "Maybe I got it wrong. I think sometimes she's scared of you."

"Lord."

"That you'll convince me to go back on the road. If she was extra testy to you earlier, that may be it," he said, closing his book. "It's in the news that you're going on tour."

"You already knew that. I asked you to join the band...out of courtesy, of course."

"And I declined...out of sanity."

"Yours or hers? Don't answer that," Randi said.

Greg chuckled. "I meant that it's out all official-like now. I hadn't told Kimberly about your offer, and she damn near freaked when she saw you trending and people commenting that maybe I'll go back on the road with you."

She glanced toward the house, spotting movement on the other side of the sliding glass doors. "I did want to talk to you about the tour," she said, and for Kimberly's benefit she raised her voice, "and I hired a drummer. I'm sorry, Greg, you're not able to rejoin the band."

Greg shifted to look back, then smiled at Randi. "I bet she offers you some iced tea."

"Should I drink it?"

"What's up, gal?"

Time to cut the bull. "Well, I didn't give you details but if you read the social feeds, you know who's behind this whole thing." When he nodded, she added, "I have reasons for accepting the offer, and I am kind of excited to perform again. I wonder, though, if it's worth the possibility of heartache."

"Are you quitting the TV work?" When Randi shook her head, Greg added, "So you play the concerts, have a good time, and you go back to *Danse*. You know the drill for tours, Randi. You won't see Derek all the time."

"Hard to say." The managers who'd succeeded Derek had made themselves scarce on her tours, as they tended to seek pleasure while on the clock. "They're filming it for a documentary. He may want camera time."

Greg sighed. "If it's going to bother you that much, back out." After a beat, he said, "But you don't want to."

"No." She meant it, not because walking away risked low ticket sales, and the likelihood Kristy wouldn't get to perform if there wasn't a big enough headliner. She missed the stage, the excitement, the crowds singing along with her.

"Are you worried more about your self-control than what Derek might try?"

"What?" Randi blinked. "You know I can't stand him. When we met for lunch after my birthday it took all my will power not to punch his stupid face." His stupid face and kissable lips like a drug, the way they paralyzed her…

Greg swung his legs around to touch the ground. Elbows on knees, he twined his fingers and leveled her with a glare. "Remember when we ran into him at that awards show, and you came close to going back to him?"

"And I walked away." Randi grimaced. "Gemini promised me a movie and soundtrack. My own *Purple Rain*."

"Which fell through because your management botched the deal," Greg finished. "You told me then you regretted giving Derek the brush off."

Randi glanced at her feet, damning her friend's steel-trap memory.

"Look me in the eye and tell me you give no thought to Derek when you're home or at work. Tell me you've lived the last thirty years in blissful neglect, happy with your every decision."

Randi looked everywhere else.

Greg chuckled and she zeroed in on him.

"Kimberly was distracting me again."

"Bullshit," she said.

Randi sighed. "I won't lie and say he's been totally out of sight, out of mind. I can't regret the last thirty years, either. My life didn't turn out the way I expected, but I'm not in a bad place. Hell, who's to say where I'd be now if I'd agreed to let Derek get me out of that Gemini contract?" She might have cut more records, and still seen disappointing sales. Been dumped by labels. Reduced to low-paying club gigs. Rock stars had shelf lives, and even Derek's genius guaranteed nothing.

"I don't believe you regret the trajectory of your professional life, Randi." Greg took her hands. "What about you?"

She smiled. "I'm never lonely, and I've never wanted for companionship."

"Bodies to warm beds are easy to find. I'm talking about love." Greg crooked his head toward the house. "Gwen's always asking when Aunt Randi's going to find somebody to marry."

"You're supposed to be raising a feminist, Greg," she warned. "Get her off those princess movies."

"How do you know she asked about getting an uncle?" He winked. "For real, Randi, you know you miss the stage. Derek has a lot riding on this, too. He's not going to do anything to fuck it up."

Derek's plea for one night together echoed in her mind. She was tougher than this, she knew. Why did his words turn her to jelly? "You're right," she said. "I guess I felt the need to talk with somebody before I go through with this. I'm a grown damn woman, and it won't be like our first tour together."

"I sure as hell don't miss it. Well, the free scotch was a nice perk. And the company." He leaned forward and kissed her forehead. "How about some spaghetti? I have no doubt Gwen invited you to stay."

They rose, and she followed him to the sliding doors. "You're sure Kimberly won't mind?"

On the other side of the glass, little Gwen was dragging a laundry basket full of toys in anticipation of her play date with Aunt Randi. Greg nodded at the scene and said, "Doesn't look like any of us have a choice, huh?"

Randi laughed and hoped her bones wouldn't creak too loudly when her goddaughter dragged her to the floor. She enjoyed the spaghetti and homemade garlic bread, played with action figures and pink sportscars, and later read one story to Gwen before Kimberly pulled her away for a bath and bed.

All in all, it was a lovely evening spent with her best friend and his family. Randi took the long way home afterward, allowing the warm feelings to remain before returning to her empty house. Never lonely, but alone. She understood Greg's words from earlier, but wasn't sure Derek should be the one to satisfy that latent need growing in her.

Once the tour started, she'd know.

Chapter Eight

"Why do people like this shite?" Derek ask aloud, watching the end credits of the first episode of *Danse Macabre*. In a span of forty minutes, Dash Gregory as the Grim Reaper had fucked three women, sucked the lifeforce from men who could have comprised the devil's football team and burned down a drugstore because the pharmacist acted like an ass. Granted, he'd looked sexy as all hell committing these deeds, and Derek had gotten some nice views of female flesh, but he thought the whole premise silly.

He tried to follow the trends in TV, binge the watercooler shows and such, but over time his late-night habits drifted back to his reliable favorites. He loved the nostalgia channels that aired classic sitcoms and cheesy sci-fi. The one he switched to now was airing an original 'where are they now' type program. Serendipity be praised, he'd landed on it as the host was talking about Randi.

"If you're a fan of *Danse Macabre*, we don't have to tell you what's become of two former teen stars. Gabby Randall and Dash Gregory are winning awards and breaking ratings records as the producer and star of ExStream's biggest hit to date. You may not realize, though, another *Wondermancer High* alumna is responsible for some of the awesome action on that show."

Derek turned up the volume.

"These days she goes by her real name as *Danse*'s lead director, but back in the eighties Randi Raucous ruled the radio waves with her hard-driving rock-and-roll style." The screen cut to a montage of Randi's early videos, most of which featured her and the band in a concert setting. The sight triggered a memory of her reluctance to participate in a 'story' video. Duncan had once suggested *Play It Safe* be set to scenes portraying Randi as a teen rebelling against her stalwart father, ending with her reconciling with the old man in tears. She'd balked, unwilling to mime to her song like that, but in the end, she'd taken the song to the label Gemini got her signed to, so it was for nothing. Derek suspected Duncan had sold another singer on the concept, because soon after everybody was talking about a clip with the same premise, one that swept the major video awards.

How weird, then, for Randi to insist she wanted to do films when they'd met up at the awards. Well, not so strange. Randi's urge to rebel was a natural instinct for her. Had he agreed she ought to make movies, she'd have resisted.

"Randi's music career started to decline when tastes in music turned from hard-pounding rock to soulful grunge. With her fourth album failing to chart in the

Hot 100, her second label dumped her and Randi traded in her guitar for movie scripts." Then came a clip from a horrid teen sex romp where Randi had played the MILF object of desire.

"Typecast as the tramp with a heart of gold, and the tough-talking biker chick du jour, Randi spent much of the nineties in a string of straight-to-video schlock flicks. It's said this role in *Season of the Bitch* — the screen cut to a shot of Randi shooting lightning bolts from her fingers to kill a would-be mugger — "attracted the attention of Will Huxley, who sought her out for the recurring role of Aunt Rowdy on a show he developed about a school for wizards, *Wondermancer High.*"

"And the rest is history," Derek muttered and reached for the remote. Blessed silence encroached upon the space between him and the set and he stretched out on his sofa. He'd learned little from the program, given that he had many contacts in the industry who'd offered news in passing of Randi over the years. Every time he'd heard of her wallowing in a career valley he'd thought to pick up the phone, but his pride had kept him from completing a call. That, and the expectation of rejection. With all this in the past, though, he had no way of knowing how she might have reacted had he offered to remove her from a set filled with fire-breathing spider monsters and put in her a studio to sing.

He closed his eyes and saw images of the *Danse Macabre* episode glowing with clarity in his mind. Good for her that the *Wondermancer* job had set her on a path that led to Gabby Randall, anyway. Randi reaped critical praise and a healthy paycheck thanks to the show, and her bosses encouraged her to return to her roots. Amid the Dash-as-Reaper mayhem playing in his head, Derek saw Gabby's face, serene with a touch of concern clouding her. He'd assured her and Lena he'd do nothing to sway Randi back to music full-time, but if Randi came to that decision alone he'd not discourage it.

Lying on his back brought on memories of being with her, holding her and kissing her after her rehearsal party. He'd picked up on her shock and gradual acceptance then, but he'd be lying to himself if he didn't admit to expecting more... What? Aggression? More desire to take control? She'd spent much of her career projecting the image of a stubborn independent. Yet she'd reacted quite like a submissive in his arms.

Does she like it rough? He stayed away from news of her personal life over the years. The links between her and select actors were bullshit, of course. Her management had concocted more than a few romances to hide this one or the other's sexuality. With JZD, she'd had no time to look, much less date, but that had happened as part of Derek's promise to the Marshes to take care of their daughter.

Now, he wanted to care for Randi as more than a musician in his employ.

Further thoughts dissolved when his phone shuddered for a few seconds. He kept notifications on social media active, and saw one of Too True's official accounts had posted a teaser trailer for the documentary. It was a minute long and consisted of footage from Randi's house, but the likes and shares were swift in coming. Randi had yet to sing one note on stage and she'd gone viral.

Her enthusiasm radiated strong from his small phone screen. Her smile turned back the clock to reveal the young rebel on live television, dancing her fingers over guitar strings like every rock legend before her. His heart panged for more than a kiss, and he pondered what she'd thought of him when he'd left his proposition hanging over her that night. They hadn't spoken beyond a few texts since.

He called up his dial pad when the phone shook in his hand. Gabby's face lit up the screen and he answered her call. "I was just watching a video," he said with chuckle.

"You liked it, I hope?" asked Gabby. "My feeds are blowing up. Everybody thinks I can get tickets for the Hollywood Bowl show."

"I can guarantee you two, at least." He groaned, understanding her situation. So many people had come out of the woodwork, acting like close buddies, though he couldn't recall meeting half of them. Tickets weren't a problem for him, and he'd make sure the true VIPs got theirs. "The video was short, but I suppose that's the point for a teaser. It worked, I can tell you that. I want to see more, and I'll be there for most of it."

"Yeah. I was a bit worried putting it out before we actually film anything, but I trust Lena. You have to create a demand and get people excited. We were promoting *Danse Macabre* before we signed Dash, so I know all about that." She laughed.

"How's Randi?" he asked.

"What, you don't know?" Gabby's mirth sounded stiffer now, confused. "Don't you two talk?"

"Well…given our history, and her feelings, we tend to get on better when we're quiet." *And in different cities.*

"Huh." She said it as commentary, not a question. "Randi likes to scold me for not trying to reach out to my parents, and here she is committing the same so-called sins." After a beat, she added, "You know, your fingers aren't broken either."

"Because I'm in a safe place."

"She can't hate you. Why go through this tour if she did?"

Derek had answers to go. Love of music. Loyalty to Kristy and Zane. Devotion to the fans. Anyone with a heart like Randi's would tour with the devil to make other people happy. There was no sense arguing with Gabby about it.

"I hope you're right," he told her, and the conversation lingered on for a few more minutes before they said goodbye. Derek moved to dial Randi but instead checked her social accounts, where he found a picture posted minutes ago of her in a selfie with Greg.

With her close friend, she smiled big and expressed her love in all caps and multiple heart emojis. Derek powered down his phone and rested back, eyes closed and hoping for the day she might do the same for him.

It lasted two seconds. He opened his eyes and held up his phone. Wishing wouldn't make the day come.

* * * *

The sharp pinging sound signaled a call. Randi tapped the button attached to the device in her right ear. "Talk to me."

"Randi?"

"Derek?" She parroted his quizzical tone.

"Are you in a wind tunnel, love?"

"I'm on my bike, talking to you on my headset." She was almost home, bone tired and looking forward to collapsing into bed. It took the long ride back, her muscles aching in this prolonged position, to remind her of her age. Despite being younger than advertised, she was still too old to sit on a floor while playing with a five-year-old. Forget bed, she needed to work out the kinks in a hot shower first.

"Should I wait until you've pulled over somewhere? This can't be safe, talking to me while you're driving."

"It's all hands-free, and L.A. traffic moves like mud. I'm fine. What do you want, Derek?" She paused behind a convertible at a red light. The air around her grew heavy with her exhaustion. She'd had such a nice time at Greg's, and even Kimberly had warmed up once she'd accepted that Randi had no ulterior motive for the visit. If Derek intended to harsh her good feelings she'd cut him off.

"It's been a few days since we talked like human beings. We're about to embark on a nationwide tour, and I thought I should check in on your well-being. I'm allowed, yes?"

"I guess." He scolded her without scolding. Everything out of his mouth took on authority when he had none to wield. She saw no point in antagonizing him. The familial harmony of the Orvilles' home still warmed her heart. "I appreciate your concern, Derek. I'm good. Rehearsals are good and we'll be ready for the first show. Don't worry about that."

"I never have. You're a professional and you put a solid band together." After a beat, he asked, "Are you back from Greg's yet?"

"How did you know… Oh." Right, she'd posted that selfie. "Well, I commend your good taste in the social media you follow."

Derek laughed. "Come over for a drink? I know you're not working tomorrow, so there's no rush to get home, is there?"

"No, except that I'm beat."

"I suggested a drink, not a marathon. Plus, I have a couch," Derek said in a near purr.

You have a bed, too. Funny he chose not to mention it. Maybe he thought she'd wreck if he propositioned her over the phone. The light turned green and she drove a few blocks to the next one. Where she stopped, she'd need to turn left to get to Derek's place, and right to go home.

"I don't know if I'd be good company," she said, and she wasn't trying to back out of a social evening. A drink sounded nice after time spent under Kimberly's alcohol-free roof, but Gwen and Pickles had put her through her paces.

"All I want is time to relax with a friend. We don't have to solve the world's problems, just sit together and smile. Enjoy the space between us."

Close the space between them, more like it. Was it possible to want something so badly and to want to run away from it? Randi gripped her handlebars and darted her eyes right and left down the cross street. One turn determined the fate of tonight, and clashing memories of their last fight and their recent kiss warred within her.

Derek was staying in a home in the Hollywood Hills owned by JZD, a modest one by the area's standards. Randi had visited it several times over the decades, more than once while he was away and somebody else had free rein for a party. It had been years since she'd last stepped foot inside, though she'd ridden past the place on the way to visit Steffi Corden, who lived close by.

Finding her way without guidance wasn't the issue. She thought about what might happen if she agreed, if she wanted to stay longer than a few hours.

A horn sounded behind her and she cursed. "Yeah, yeah," she muttered and rolled into a nearby parking lot.

"Randi, you there?"

"Yes, just thinking." Home was closer, and safe. Nothing there but her empty bed and a pint of ice cream, plus a few toys in her nightstand drawer. They worked in a pinch, but she preferred a warm body to something made in a factory.

Derek, too close for comfort even miles away from her home, caused her body and brain to battle. *We hate him, we want him, we'd rather burn out batteries getting off…*

We want to know what might have been.

"You okay, love?"

"Yeah. I'll see you in a few."

* * * *

Derek greeted her with a filled highball glass fizzing with cola and bourbon. "You never let me drink on tour," she said, taking a sip. "Is that still a rule?"

"I think you can make that decision for yourself now. Anyway, you were underage at the time. I had it figured out then. Even if you weren't, I had promised your father to keep you sober."

Randi shrugged. "Never stopped other people. I've seen them try to ply children with booze at parties."

"Yes, I've been reading all the exposés coming out. Bloody disgusting." It was one reason why Derek's father refused to manage minors, though Derek had argued maybe they could provide a safe space. Da never wanted the hassle of it, however. Randi, in her youth, remained the sole exception to that rule.

"Try being the operative word here," Randi said. "I used to go places with Gabby and the other kids for publicity for the show. Every time somebody came their way with a joint or a vial of blow I chased them in the other direction."

"Good for you, and them. Anyway, if there's anything you want added to the tour rider speak now while I can still have it done. Legal, that is."

"Eh, I'm pretty low maintenance these days, and I don't need anything to impair my playing." She stepped deeper into the house and scanned the living room. He wasn't sure when she'd last visited, but some touches had stayed the same since the eighties. The mantel over the fireplace held an array of music industry trophies, and gold and platinum records lined the walls. Every direction they turned, something glinted back.

She sat on the sofa while Derek took the opposite end. "I used to call this room Fort Knox for all the gold plating," she said, then laughed. "Bit pretentious having all this hardware out, you think?"

"No." Derek shook his head, glancing at the achievements of his firm's clients. "Nothing wrong with showing some pride for your talent." He studied her, admiring the wind-blown, fresh-from-the-freeway look in her hair and flushed skin. "How come you didn't have your records out at home?"

"Oh, well." She didn't meet his stare and instead kept the glass to her lips for a long moment before elaborating. "I let my folks hang on to those. They seemed happy to show them off to friends, so why not?"

"Yes," he said, trying to draw out more, "but they've since passed and you got them back, right?" He recalled seeing the nomination certificate for that Best Director award. *Why display that and nothing else?*

"For a while." She nodded, and added in a lower voice, "Until I sold them."

"What? Why?"

Randi's expression turned sour, almost mournful. "I had a few bad years between breaking off with Gemini and working on *Wondermancer High*. Royalties were slow in coming, the movies I did paid scale and barely covered the rent, and I wasn't about to expect relatives to help with bills." She barked out a bitter laugh. "Especially when all the cousins were still coming to me with their hands out."

"I'm sorry, love."

"Don't be. Everything's worked out since." She took a deep drink, coughing a bit as the alcohol burned down her throat. The mood in the room had turned down a dim path as she remembered her leaner days, and relatives who'd treated her like an ATM. She'd rid herself of all the toxic people in her life once it had gotten back on track, and that had helped.

So now she had a nice home, a good supplemental income from residuals from *Wondermancer High* and the better films she'd made, plus the tour…yet the hollowness in her heart remained. What was missing?

Her attention had turned away from Derek for a moment, long enough for her to drop her guard. She blinked when his hand dipped low and crossed her line of vision. He caressed her cheek.

"What's wrong? You look so unhappy all of a sudden."

"I don't know. I was having such a great day. I saw Greg and had dinner with them. I'm going back on tour… I guess thinking about the bad times makes me nervous, like they'll come back."

"You know you can come to me any time if you need help. Money, support, anything."

She nodded. Of course she knew, even when they'd gone for years without talking. She knew if she picked up a phone or dashed off an email, he'd show with his hands out, to lift her up.

She'd never called, though. She'd wanted to forge her independence, her ability to make good decisions.

The idea of his unflinching support, coupled with her long resentment of him thanks to her bullheaded nature, proved too much for the moment. The first tear burned a trail down her cheek and she wiped it away. Soon his arms enveloped her, and she let herself be drawn to his body.

Damn that woodsy cologne of his. Whatever it was called, it should be renamed Derek because the scent would forever trigger memories of him.

Derek smoothed a hand down her back and brushed his lips against her ear. "I don't want you to think I'm trying to take advantage here," he said. "I've always wanted your happiness. Sue me if I believe it's right there for you onstage."

"I'm not leaving Gabby for good," she said. "I adjusted my work schedule for this, but I'm going back." They'd had to move up shooting the Steffi Corden episodes in order to have material to tease the spinoff series. She'd handled it like a pro.

"I'm not asking you to, love. You are the architect of your career now, and you're doing well."

She huffed. "This some kind of reverse psychology?" His touch singed through her leather jacket. *Stuffy in here now...*

"It's a friend complimenting another friend. Take from it whatever you wish." Her 'friend's' lips brushed the shell of her right ear. "You smell amazing."

Liar. Who got turned on by garlicky pasta sauce and Play-Doh? She opened her mouth to ask that when he captured her in a hungry kiss. Bourbon and sugar overtook the taste of tonight's dinner and he switched from caressing her jacket to trying to remove it.

'Give me the favor...' Was this it, the favor? Was it happening now? She tried to remember, had he asked for it once or at least once?

He slipped his hands under her shirt and moved up her back. Warm to the touch, he fiddled with her bra clasp as though he'd unclipped it a hundred times. The elastic keeping the girls in place sprang loose and soon after that he moved his fingers around to cup her flesh.

He lowered his face down as he pushed away her T-shirt. "You are so beautiful, Randi," he said. She gasped, not so much from the contact of his lips on her swell of one breast, but at the sound of her name. He'd called her 'love', that very English term of endearment, almost since day one. She used to think it made him come off as a stereotype from a British comedy, but in time she'd come to like it because nobody else had a name like that for her. It had taken years for her parents to concede to calling her Randi instead of her given name.

Now, Derek's mouth was too busy to say anything. His tongue stroked her nipple to peak hardness before moving to the next one. The nerves he set off fired through her veins and down her spine, and he worked the waist of her jeans, adding to her mounting frustration. They sat side by side on the sofa, and it left little comfort for seduction. They needed to lie down if they were to continue kissing and tugging at each other's clothes.

Speaking of which…he was way ahead of her. Derek had on a black turtleneck and khakis, still intact on his body. What to reach for first, though?

He gave her little time to decide. He pecked her lips again and his arms crushed her harder against his chest. They kissed with feverish longing, as though starving for withheld affection and taking everything offered before it vanished. Randi closed her eyes and let Derek guide her on top of him as he lay back on the couch.

She heard clasps and buckles coming undone, and zipper teeth parting. Derek tore away from her long enough to pull his shirt over his head and toss it in one corner. Randi got her fill in the few seconds before they resumed their clinch, admiring his toned physique that belied his age.

"Randi," he said again, kissing the corner of her mouth.

"Mmm."

"In about five seconds you're going to hate me."

Lord, what now? Several possibilities raced through her mind. He had to go to the bathroom, he was impotent, he was expecting his actual date to arrive soon. A quick slip of her hand on the hardened bulge in his khakis eliminated one of those, and the other two seemed ridiculous. That left…

"I don't have anything, that is —"

Randi slid her mouth across his cheek, talking without breaking kissing contact. "You invite me here, get me hornier than a senior on prom night, knowing you got nothing?"

"Well, it's not like I anticipated this part." Yet, the fact they were short on 'party hats', as a tune from her peak decade had once called them, did little to discourage Derek from pushing her jeans over her hips.

"So what's your Plan B?" she asked, and bit back a yelp when he squeezed her thigh and his ring band pinched her skin.

"I dunno. There are other…things. Other ways to have a good time." His body shook with quiet laughter as he held her. "I'd be lying if I said I'd be happy with just a cuddle tonight, though."

"We don't have to stop there." Her voice deepened with her growing confidence. "I'm clean. I've tested negative." The last time she'd taken the test, anyway, and media reports of her love life of late were greatly exaggerated. Her longtime companion these days was her job. "I'm also on the shot."

"Good to know," he murmured, and his thigh brushed her. She sensed a return to life and enthusiasm down south. "I am as well. Clean, that is, not on birth control."

"Good to know." *Ah, romance.*

Few words followed their unspoken mutual consent. What she heard in between kisses came out in whispered gasps and grunts, endearments like love and baby and yes. Air cooled her skin more with each item of clothing discarded, and her body reacted well ahead of her brain. It hadn't registered in her mind that she was about to fuck Derek until she straddled him while naked on his couch and seated herself fully on him.

Worth it? taunted her conscience. Was this moment worth a decades-long gap in communications? Would she have enjoyed being with Derek as nubile nympho — tighter around the tummy, less bleach in her hair — more than making love close to middle age? She rocked over Derek, centering on the sensation of his cock inside her, and watched his reaction. His eyes seemed intent on locking with hers for the entire ride, holding her attention and emotion.

His hands, all the while, rested on her hips and helped to guide her speed. He liked it fast, and she leaned forward to keep the momentum going, through a slow-building rise to a powerful orgasm. Her eyelids fluttered shut and she held on to the good feeling as long as possible, tightening her muscles around him. Her eyes shot open at the sound of his grunting release.

Relaxing a bit, she slid down until she lay flush against Derek. Their legs twined and she laid her head on his heaving chest for a moment, breathing deep as his heart drummed in her ear. It had happened so fast, the foreplay and the sex, yet her body weighed heavy with fatigue. She had trouble lifting her head, she was that tired. Not out of shape, more like exhausted in every respect.

Had they taken their time, made love like in some sexy romance movie, it might have rendered her comatose.

Derek's breathing slowed his pulsing body and he kissed the top of her head. "Stay tonight, Randi," he said. "Much as I love rutting like a teenager, I'd rather hold you all night and have another go at it later."

"You certain you can?"

He scoffed. "I'm not that old. I figured I did rather well without medicinal help, you think?"

"I didn't mean it like that," she said, and planted the heels of her hands on either side of him to push herself upward. "I hate to say I'm feeling my age."

"Your true one, or the one everybody believes you are?"

"Ass." Randi put a foot on the floor and heaved to stand. Derek managed a playful slap on her bottom before she stepped away to find her clothes. "I would like to stay, but —"

Derek propped up on his elbows. Sweaty and spent, he rocked the fresh-fucked look. Randi thought about staying and doing more, exploring more of his body and returning the favor, but instead clutched her underwear and pressed her thighs together. Staying would make it harder to leave, and she had a life beyond this house.

This tour, her music, her former manager.

She'd perform the shows, and when it ended, they ended. She'd conceded to the lovemaking part early, got that out of the way. Nothing left to do but sing.

Right?

Derek frowned at her, looking concerned. He sat up and reached a hand out to her. "You okay, love? You went a touch white there."

Randi came back to the moment and exhaled. "I'm fine," she said, and looped her legs back into her underwear. "I should go."

"You don't have to. I know you're off tomorrow. Stay."

"Not exactly. I have a second job now, and I have to rehearse for it." She gave him a pointed look. "I'm at about ninety percent with the setlist. I won't go out on any stage and give less than a hundred."

"You never did." Derek smiled. Randi had trouble meeting his eyes as they talked. His cock, hanging between his legs as he sat, seemed to thicken and lengthen. Maybe it was her imagination, or wishful thinking, but *'another go at it'* tempted her. "And you know I'd never do anything to impede your career."

Was he talking about her TV work or the music? Randi got her jeans on and scanned the carpet for her bra. "Then you'll understand I want to get a good night's sleep and be ready for the band."

"Yes." No protests, no pushed-out lower lip to show disappointment. Derek stood and drew her into an embrace. The skin-on-skin attention brought a shiver down her back as they kissed.

"We'll have plenty of time during the tour," he whispered, then moved away to let her finish dressing.

"Sure." The word slipped out before she had time to process a response. Derek remained in his altogether while he fixed another drink, leaving her to fumble with her bra and wonder if she should make time for him on the road.

She'd told him she never wanted to see him again afterward. Could she enjoy being in his bed and still want that?

Chapter Nine

1984

"Is this all for me?"

Randi dropped her duffel bag just inside the spacious hotel suite. In her awed mind, it stretched out for a mile, all plush carpet and cream walls. A sitting area with a leather sectional curved around a big-screen television that took up one corner, across from a stocked wet bar. Beyond that, a king bed sat on a platform and overlooked an expansive window separating her from an unobstructed view of Lake Michigan.

Without waiting for Derek's answer, she moved deeper into the room, tempted to belly flop onto the bed and breaststroke the fluffy comforter into a jumbled mess. If it turned out the hotel had made a mistake and led her into some foreign dignitary's suite, maybe they'd concede to let her keep it if she got comfortable.

A girl can dream. It was a silly idea, more so than the notion she was afraid to touch anything. Her surroundings were elegant and high-class, reserved for a big star.

"You belong here, Randi. Never doubt it."

She turned to see Derek at the bar, grabbing a soda from the mini-fridge. "That can probably costs ten dollars," she said. "Be cheaper to go to the drugstore across the street."

"Oh, live a little, love. Here." He popped it open before handing it over. It tasted no more special at ten dollars a can.

"You have a few hours to yourself before dinner," he told her. They were meeting executives from the label's Chicago offices at some steakhouse named for a Cub or Bear or whatever. "Enjoy the pay movies and honor bar. Send up for dessert if you want, but get a good night's sleep for tomorrow."

"Of course." The morning show, *A.M. Chicago*. It was bigger than *Donahue* now in this market, so Randi was told, due to the increasing popularity of its new female host. "You think they'll be into my music?" she asked. "I don't really see these songs as something the morning crowd will like."

"Why do you say that?" Derek took back the can and set it on the nightstand, using a visitors' guide brochure as a coaster.

"Old people watch morning shows." Randi drifted toward the window. "Teenagers like m —" *Shit*. Almost slipped and implicated herself. "Teenagers don't get up till past noon in the summertime if they don't have jobs."

"You'll be great, love. This new host has a great ear and eye for good product. She's an influencer, and with people videotaping morning shows now you stand to reach a bigger audience. All the grandchildren of those 'old people'."

Nice, so now I'm a product. Not a human being. She felt like a slab of cellophane-wrapped meat, on display in the specials bin. Derek must have noticed some hesitance in her expression, as he came forward with a placating smile.

He kissed her forehead. The feather-soft touch of his lips singed her, and she held her breath. "Trust me, okay? There's a progression to all of this. You'll be performing for the hip late-night crowds soon enough." Without another word he padded to the door and it snicked shut behind him.

She had no idea which room was his in this gargantuan high-rise hotel. Hell, had he even left a key in case she locked herself out?

"Guess I have no choice but to trust you," she said to the walls, then jumped backward onto the bed and sank into the down-soft comforter, alone on a cloud of luxury.

* * * *

Present Day

"Is this all mine?"

Randi retained little memory of the last time she'd visited Tulsa. She'd opened for Black Alchemy there, and they'd crashed in a low-star motor lodge until a roadie banged on her door at ass crack o'clock to get on the bus. In her mind, every date on the tour featured the same thin-walled room with stiff, floral-print sheets and no cable TV. Even when she'd headlined back in the day, she'd had to go outside to get her own ice. It was a far cry from that luxury Chicago hotel when Derek had showed her off to the label's satellite offices.

Back in Tulsa for the first date of the Eighties Ladies show — sold out, at that — Randi marveled at the posh digs. Her suite had a king bed facing a flat screen, plus a mini kitchen with a huge gourmet gift basket wrapped in colored cellophane.

"Bit much for one night, you think?" she asked as she set her backpack on the coffee table in the corner sitting area. Everything smelled clean and looked new, a complete one-eighty from the stained hovels she'd suffered during career valleys. A memory of spending one night close to freezing because she'd slept on top of a bedspread with cigarette burns on it surfaced, and she shook her head.

"I wouldn't get accustomed to it, though you certainly deserve the five-star treatment." Derek moved from behind her to check the tags attached to the baskets. "We thought you all ought to have a nice place for your first show. The accommodations will be more, ah, economy class until we get back to L.A."

Made sense. With the addition of the film crew, it meant more people to feed and house. "Fine by me. They all look the same in the dark with my eyes closed, anyway." Derek had placed the room keycards on the sink counter and she grabbed both. It occurred to her that Derek might ask her for one, but she wasn't certain she wanted him to have access to her room. In the time between their night together and now, they hadn't made love again. During rehearsals and meetings about the tour, neither of them had mentioned it. Of course, Lena had cameras trained on them at every available second to capture material for the docuseries, and Randi wasn't about to admit on film that she'd shagged the boss.

She stared at the cards in her hand while Derek prattled on about schedules and dinner, and sorted her feelings. She'd enjoyed the hell out of the sex, and given the opportunity she'd take Derek back to bed. Why not enjoy a fling while on the road? They were both single adults, owed nobody any explanations, and she wasn't dead yet. She couldn't understand, though, why deeper thoughts about it made her uneasy.

Saying goodbye to Derek after the last concert… Was that it? She wanted that, though. Get the lust out of her system, go back to Too True and conquer a new TV series. Derek could go back to his agency and focus on getting somebody else to trend on Twitter.

She looked up and a curse echoed in her head. Derek watched her, waiting for her to answer a question she hadn't heard. She tried to speak when Kristy rescued her by barging through the open door with a gift basket of her own.

"Did you get one, too? Look at all this." The woman turned the prize around in her arms, giddy like nobody had ever given her anything in her life. "This chocolate popcorn looks amazing, and I know you don't like stuff like that. I'll trade you the cookies for it."

Grateful for the moment of levity, Randi let out a short laugh and fetched her basket. "Fine by me, but don't be scarfing that stuff down before you go on. You don't need to choke on a popcorn husk in front of thirty thousand people."

Kristy gave a stuttering laugh, one implying a release of nerves. "You'll be fine, just like riding a bike," Randi added by way of consolation. She wanted to mention how long it had been since she'd performed on stage, but figured if she opened her mouth Derek would interject. She was jittery about tonight as well — no need to add pressure with more platitudes.

"I never learned to ride a bike," Kristy muttered. "Too much time on tour buses. Never needed one." She laughed.

Derek pocketed his phone and passed both women toward the door. "I'll be next door if you need me, ladies. Get some rest and be ready to motor in about three hours for sound checks." With a wink, he was out of the door and Randi closed it behind him.

"I wish I had his confidence." Kristy stabbed at the cellophane until she poked a hole through it. She pulled a chocolate truffle out with two fingers. "I mean, I've rehearsed, and Zane knows the music, and we sound great in the garage, but he hasn't done anything bigger than a nightclub in — "

"I slept with Derek."

Kristy looked up from unwrapping her treat, then at the made bed. "But we just got here."

"Not today," Randi snapped. "Back home, a few weeks ago." She reached for her gift basket and perused the contents. The comforting tang of a dark chocolate truffle might help to soothe her, but she saw herself devouring all the goodies before Derek returned. He didn't need to discover her in the corner of her suite, groaning and on the edge of a sugar coma.

"Ohh, I see." Kristy waggled her eyebrows. "I suppose that was like riding a bike for you. How long's it been?"

"Cute." She set the basket aside and helped herself to the minibar instead. She opened a pre-mixed margarita and took a quick pull from the can, wincing at the tart taste. "He hasn't brought it up since that night, and I get the sense he's biding his time, you know? Like he's waiting for me to drop my guard before he strikes again."

"Strikes? Randi, you make him sound like one of these sexual predators in the news. Derek's one of the good guys." Kristy frowned. "You saying he forced himself?"

Randi shook her head. "No, it's all been mutual. He did tell me he wanted to get together before the tour ended...and we say goodbye for good."

"Why would he say that? Derek's held a torch for you for years. He might not admit it, but you can see it from space. You can't tell me you still don't have some feelings for him, either," Kristy said before her attention diverted toward the door. Noise and laughter filtered through the wall, and she moved for a peek into the hall.

"It was kind of my idea," Randi said. She glimpsed Zane through the gap in the doorway, chatting with his drummer. She recognized a third person as part of Lena's team, and she closed the door. One eavesdropped word might inspire him to grab a camera and capture a juicy offstage conversation. She'd agreed to being filmed, but the world didn't need to know about this.

"Randi, we've known each other since the Stone Age," Kristy said. "I know the whole story, both sides of it. At the risk of pissing you off, I have to ask — do you truly believe Derek is at fault for anything that caused all this ill will?"

Randi loved her friend, admired her preference for setting tact aside and cutting through the bullshit. The thought to remind her of Kristy's less than prudish behavior back in the day passed. That would be a deflective tack and Kristy didn't deserve to be slut shamed.

"I liked him, I was legal and he slept with some hack comedienne," Randi said.

"You were his client, he kept things professional."

"He wanted to control the songs I recorded, what I performed live..."

"You mean he was doing his job?" Kristy arched an eyebrow.

"Hey. Managers and clients hook up all the time. They get married."

"They get divorced, too. Derek believed in your talent enough to not want to fuck it up with romantic drama." Kristy unwrapped a second truffle but handed it to her. "I'm not taking sides here."

"You fooled me." Randi bit hard. Coconut. She winced.

"You and Derek are two of my favorite people. I like to think you're ready to let go of the past and consider what good awaits you in the future if you let it." Kristy clutched her basket, the cookie and popcorn trade forgotten, and started for the door. "A lot of people thought Zane and I wouldn't last a year, and look at us. Amazing what can happen if you're willing to be mature about it."

I am mature, Randi wanted to protest. *Independent, used to calling the shots.* Yielding to Derek risked the control she enjoyed.

A knock surprised them, and Kristy opened the door to allow Zane and Derek into the room. Zane kissed his wife and steered her away, but not before extracting a promise to celebrate together after the show. He nodded toward Randi's minibar. "You're buying."

Randi set down the key cards and moved to open the fridge. "Help yourself. The canned margarita is nasty. I'd rather find a liquor store for something palatable."

"How about we get through the show before we start self-medicating, eh?" Derek moved to block Zane from the booze and smiled at the other man to show no hard feelings. "I know it's been a while for everybody, but you're all going to be just fine."

Zane puffed up his chest. "Hey, when have you ever known me to not act like a professional on the job?" He then held up his hand. "You know what, don't answer that." With a wordless gesture to Kristy, he escorted his wife into the hall, leaving Randi to drain her margarita into the sink.

"You okay, love?" Derek asked. "You need anything from me?"

I can think of something. Sex might soothe her nerves, but if she hit a high note in the sack it could work too well. She needed to focus on music first.

He edged closer. "What's that smile? Like you lapped up the last of the cream."

Terrific. He'd read her face. "Nothing. I want to lie down a bit. I won't get the chance later, probably."

"See you in a bit." He kissed her cheek and, grinning wide, closed her door behind him. He had things to sort out before the show, she knew. She shouldn't feel dejected that he didn't suggest sex himself.

Randi glanced at the table and gift basket and noticed a keycard missing. *The sly son of a bitch.*

She smiled.

* * * *

Hearing the crowd, watching Randi shred through a solo while her bassist swayed in time with her, one wouldn't believe thirty years had passed since her debut. Derek was rooted to one spot for her entire set, closing his eyes at various points. Her voice, the chords, the overall sound of the Randi Raucous act took him back in time. He expected to open his eyes and see the world in 1985 again.

They almost got it right. But for the multitude of lighted phones held in the air to record this moment for posterity, or some streaming app, he'd think he'd stepped into a time warp. Randi's original logo took up the giant screen behind the band, and Randi herself… Damn, but her enthusiasm melted away the age. She'd looked terrific regardless, but something about singing and playing the guitar preserved her youth, made her near immortal. Derek was glad they had cameras poised on tonight's concert. He'd show her the raw footage and prove once and for all that she belonged in front of a crowd.

So far, the entire show had been amazing. Not one hiccup during any of the acts. It wasn't uncommon to experience a gaffe like a flubbed lyric or an issue with sound or lighting at the start of a tour, and Derek hoped this served as a sign of better things to come. It didn't irk him to see people snapping short videos to upload online. Let the world see Randi Raucous wasn't some old-school has-been.

"Good night, Tulsa, thank you!" she shouted into her mic as she strummed the final chords of *Play It Safe*. Finishing with a high-kick, she gathered the band together for a unified bow and ran offstage to a deafening roar of approval. One by one, each grabbed a proffered towel or bottle of water and basked in the platitudes from friends and crew. Brad let out a rebel yell and hooked his arm around his son's neck, and rewarded him with a noogie.

"Yeah! That's how you get it done!" Derek smiled at the sight while Randi cackled her approval. The show's energy transferred easily to the festive backstage atmosphere. Everybody was on a natural high with no signs of coming down.

Randi draped her arms around Derek's neck and hugged him tight. "I guess you can tell me you told me so. This was so amazing," she said. "I feel like I could sing all night."

"Just one more song," he said, referring to the encore. For this setlist, Randi had insisted on a cover hit, a personal favorite. The tune rocked, and she'd longed to perform it live. Judging from the synchronized clapping of the crowd, it appeared they could go out and sing *I'm a Little Teapot* and bring down the house.

As more people swelled close to congratulate the band, Derek lost track of Randi. After a minute or so of loud chatter and sweat and heat he saw her on the fringe of the gathering, waving her band together. "Come on, let's do this. One for the road so I can hit that swimming pool of a tub back at the hotel."

"You got a tub?" Gary nudged her. "We're all sharing the janitor's closet."

"Funny. Move it."

Sticks and guitars in hand, the band jogged back onstage to a surge of cheers. Randi waited on the lip for a few seconds, took a deep breath and walked out. Derek had hoped to say something beforehand, but Randi looked too in a zone to focus on anything but her performance. No matter, he'd save his praise for later.

He stuck his hand in his jeans pocket and brushed his thumb over the keycard he'd taken from her room. He shouldn't have done it, had no right to, but he enjoyed being close to Randi, more than they'd ever been. They hadn't discussed their lovemaking since the night it happened, and he didn't want that to signal her lack of interest. By the end of the tour, he wanted at least one more night with her, if not all of them.

"All right, Tulsa!" Randi's voice projected throughout the venue. "How about one more before the noise ordinance hits?" She nodded toward Brad Junior to begin the count, and in that short gap Derek heard the chant gaining momentum from the front rows, rippling back like a wave.

"Do. It. Again. Do. It. Again…"

He watched Randi for a change in body language. She'd heard it despite the speaker in her ear connecting her to the sound engineers. Derek stood far enough away to make reading her face a challenge, and when he glanced up at the screen he saw the large projection of Randi, unsmiling and hesitant.

"Do. It. Again. Do. It. Again…" They wanted the hit. Of course they did. Randi Raucous had been on fire tonight, and to hear her biggest song would cap off a perfect night. These people didn't know her history with the song, though, or her aversion to it. They were fans acting as fans should.

Randi, until now playing the role of rock star, now appeared off her game. Brad and Gray closed in on her. Nobody played their instruments. The three of them seemed in an awkward huddle while the crowd grew restless.

Kristy came up beside Derek. "What's going on? Why isn't she singing?"

"The crowd's thrown her for a loop. She can't shake it off." Derek willed her to gain strength and to proceed. Sing something. If they at least started *Crossroads*, it would appease the audience and perhaps lead them to think they were getting that song in addition to *Do It Again*. Then Randi could beat a hasty retreat and be in the car before the lights came on.

No music started. Gary looked in Derek's direction, his face ashen and eyebrows raised in question. Those poor men didn't know what to do with their leader down.

"How's your voice?" Derek asked Kristy.

"Huh?" Her direction turned from the stage to him. "I'm good. Better than I'd thought I'd be."

"You up for one more?"

"Sure."

"Grab Zane." He then barked at Brad's tech to get a guitar and tapped a roadie to follow him onstage.

The crowd's cheers mellowed in volume a bit with their presence, then gave way to wailing and gasps as Randi collapsed. Derek managed to catch her before she hit the ground.

* * * *

No nightcap in the jetted tub in the luxury suite. No chocolate-covered popcorn. None that she recalled, anyway. Either she'd gotten so wasted after the Tulsa show that it had erased her memory of an awesome afterparty, or she'd really blacked out. Last she remembered, she was standing onstage while the crowd's chanting triggered her anxiety, and the next moment she was waking up in her private coach.

Private in name only, of course. For this trip, she shared the bus with some of Lena's camera crew. One of them had a lens stuck in her face when her eyes opened.

She glanced at the red-light indicator and scowled at its owner. "I am going to shove that thing up your ass," she ground out.

Skippy, whatever the hell his name was, lowered the camera and simpered toward the back. Randi reminded herself to talk to Lena about the day's footage. For a moment, she thought to request that part stay in the final cut. Let people have a nice laugh.

Blech. She tasted cotton and bile, but suffered no headache. That ruled out a hangover. When she moved to sit up her head spun for a few seconds, but she recovered and stepped from her bed platform into the aisle. Her clothes sagged a bit and she realized she no longer had on her concert outfit but baggy flannel pajama pants, a raglan and socks with rubber grips on the soles. *Who changed my clothes while I slept? What else was done?*

Putting one foot before the other, she grasped seatbacks and luggage rails for balance until she reached the mini-fridge. Voices behind a curtained section alerted her to Derek, working the spin machine hard. A question, tinny and presumably from a female reporter, asked about possible cancellations.

"No. The tour is going on as planned," Derek said. Randi peered through the curtains to see he was holding his phone with the screen turned to the ceiling, his neck bent forward as he spoke into the microscopic mic. "Randi has no health problems to cause concern. Last night's gaffe was borne of a bit of excitement. We were all focused on putting on a good show. Randi simply did not hydrate enough. It's an issue we're in the process of correcting."

"Are you saying Randi's on an IV right now?"

The fuck? Randi sulked back to her napping area to put distance between her and the interview, lest she barge in to set whoever straight. She'd passed out onstage, and that embarrassed her. She'd drink more water if she had to, but she sure as hell wasn't near death like the media wanted to sell.

She cracked open the can of ginger ale from the fridge and, after a long pull to wash last night from her mouth, set it in a cupholder while she lay back. Her bag hung from a hook close by and she fished for her phone, which had blown up with texts and notifications. Most came from concerned friends, others from media requesting quotes. She cleared away the latter and opened her news app, and winced at the flashing headline from the first featured site.

IS RANDI'S ROCK OFF? screamed the headline of one gossip blog. She saw the attempt to play on her name, but it looked weak to her. She learned nothing new from the report, either, aside from Kristy and Zane stepping in to perform the encore with her band while roadies carted her to someplace safe. Nothing about a doctor or emergency room, leaving Randi to assume Derek had her taken straight to the bus to sleep off her anxiety.

Of course, the demand to hear *Do It Again* had caused all of this. She glanced at the time on her phone and was amazed to see how long she'd had to sleep it off. A quick survey of her social accounts let her know how many fans wished her well. The majority of the messages bade her to recover soon, in time for the dates for which they had tickets. A few trolls snarked at her to give up, but Randi paid them no mind.

Kristy and Zane playing her encore, though…that hurt a bit. Not that she thought either of her friends incapable of entertaining, but knowing they'd had to cover for her left Randi feeling inadequate.

"How are you, love? Better?"

Her heart spasmed at the sound of Derek's voice, and she mashed the Home button on her phone, as though she'd been caught doing something wrong. "I'm good. Where are we?"

"Almost to Lincoln. We'll check in, and you and Kathy have a remote interview after lunch."

"Right. Did nobody want to try to revive me, so I could at least dress myself?" She looked out of the window to see the sun high the in the sky.

The platform bed dipped and rocked, and she rolled back as Derek joined her. He pulled the privacy curtain and stretched one arm to draw her close. He smelled of strong coffee and tobacco. She knew he'd given up smoking several years ago, and guessed last night's fiasco had brought on this lapse of bad habits. The last thing she'd wanted to do was cause problems.

"Randi, you were exhausted. I thought at first your fainting had to do with the crowd clamoring for that song, but when I got to you, your skin was clammy and pale. You didn't look right."

"So why am I not waking up in a hospital?"

"We moved you to first aid at the venue. You weren't on drugs, and as you have no history of diabetes or other illness the EMTs didn't think you needed it. Just told us to make sure you hydrate and eat well so it doesn't happen again." Derek brushed his lips against her forehead. "You came to while we were breaking down the stage."

"Yeah?" No memory of it. Not even a fuzzy picture in her head.

"We gave you water. You were tired, so we smuggled you back to the hotel until it was time to leave. Kristy and Kathy changed your clothes, by the way."

Randi laughed. "Thirty years ago, Kathy got drunk and told me she wanted to get into my pants. Hope it worth the wait."

"I promise you, nothing untoward occurred from the time you fell and now," Derek said. "I am sorry you don't remember that short moment of consciousness. We were doing what we thought best."

"For me or the tour?"

"Randi, you know I would never put you at risk." Derek sounded hurt.

"I know." She wanted to lash out, put blame on somebody besides herself. She took care of her body as she could, but the time leading up to the tour had seen her binging on soda and protein bars instead of substantial meals. The overtime she'd put into *Danse Macabre* and *Fallen Angel* before she'd left had had a bad effect on her as well, but she'd refused to leave any loose ends before this trip.

She'd passed out because she'd tried to do too much. At least now she could relax a bit and enjoy the subsequent shows, but she knew more than Lena's cameras were watching her every move.

"I'm a bit hungry. What's left to eat here?" She reached for the ginger ale.

"How about a cashew bar? Something to tide you over until after the interview."

"Sure. I don't need to be throwing up on Kathy's shoes on live TV." She squirmed as though to get off the bed, but Derek surprised her by producing a granola and nut bar from his jacket pocket. Providence, or maybe he was keeping an eye on her as she suspected? She thanked him as she peeled away the wrapper.

"How come Kristy isn't doing the interview?" she asked. "She saved my butt last night. You'd think she'd ought to be on TV as well."

"You really think that's a good idea?" Derek frowned. "It would take the attention away from you, create more PR around last night's incident."

Translation — no drama. It struck Randi as odd, seeing as how television fare thrived on it, regardless of the show. Besides, what was the saying about there being no such thing as bad publicity? In her eyes, talk about the Tulsa show could boost sales for the rest of the tour. People would come out to see what, if anything, happened next.

Anyway, Kristy was the first act, but an important one. She deserved the same treatment she and Kathy enjoyed. It burned Randi to think her friend might miss out on exposure, and she said as much to Derek. "Think about her future," she added. "When this tour's over she might decide to go back into music on a serious level. Do club dates with Zane or even on her own."

Derek scoffed, and Randi guessed the response forming in his mind, that he managed to keep unsaid. *At her age?* Hell, Kristy wasn't that much older than her, and plenty of performers their age and older embarked on longer, more rigorous schedules than this. Why not Kristy cutting another album and going on the road to support it?

"If she comes on TV, it's not going to slight me," Randi said. "She and I are closer than I am to Kathy, anyway. I want her there."

Derek sighed, a long and defeated sound that motivated him off the platform and to a standing position. Leaning on the edge of the thin mattress, he stared at her. "It's not that I don't think Kristy will leapfrog you," he said, "but this is your tour. You should get as much PR as you're offered."

Randi turned on her side, head propped on her elbow. "It's the Eighties Ladies tour. Ladies, plural." With that, she snatched at the curtain to hide his face.

"I'll see what I can do," he said through the filmy sheet.

"Good boy."

She made to close her eyes when the curtain whipped to one side and Derek dove down for a quick kiss. "Take care of yourself, love," he whispered. "I wouldn't like to lose you a second time, for good." He disappeared before she got a word out in reply.

Chapter Ten

Spring, 2001

"So it's come to this," Randi murmured, shaking off a chill from the echo chamber of the chilly hotel ballroom. All around her, people either pushed handcarts heavy with cardboard boxes or set up banner stands and tablecloths for their personal spaces. She used to side-eye events likes these, the mass cattle-call autograph shows featuring actors and other celebrities of fading relevance. Airport hotels in Los Angeles held them all the time. Her father had attended a few when he'd worked in the entertainment industry, to support to support friends selling glossies and books.

Snarky Randi Marsh had scoffed at 'those people' — former pinups beset with stretch marks and wrinkles, ex-child stars who'd failed to take stardom into adulthood, singers milking their one hit. Never had she thought she'd come to one of these as an exhibit for people to gawk at, but here she was.

She needed the money, and Scream Break Weekend in Cherry Hill, New Jersey, had offered her a decent appearance fee—more than what others here were getting, she'd learned. She had to perform for the extra cash, though, so it was some comfort she could view this gig as an actual concert and not a career nadir.

"Heyyy, Randi Raucous. Lookin' good, sugar."

Her blood curdled, but she put on a smile to greet the short, flame-haired slick boy standing at her table. A man, of course, but he appeared to maintain a youthful look. He wore a jacket over a black shirt with a tuxedo front print, jeans and sneakers. The jacket sleeves were rolled up in some throwback to nineties fashion, and though Randi had no clue as to his identity she assumed somebody here had booked him since he had access to the room before it opened to the public.

He gestured to the table across from hers. "Looks like we're row buddies, huh? That is so cool. Usually I get stuck staring at some bloated wrestler for eight hours. But you...your music videos got me through puberty."

"Thanks." How else to respond to that? *I'm flattered you found me an attractive enough masturbatory fantasy. Would you like to buy an autographed picture?*

Right, the pictures. She reached for a box by her feet. It contained fifty glossies of her earliest publicity shots. She'd signed similar pictures for restaurants and record stores, any place with a wall of fame. Those she gave away, writing off the expense on her taxes. The event organizers had advised she bring a few hundred, but the initial investment worried her. She already had a ton of unsold CDs and DVDs of her crap movies in her garage, and she hoped they moved today. She'd accepted the invitation here because, unlike other conventions, this one had a policy that required attendees to purchase something if they wanted an autograph.

With the music, she rationalized people were getting something they could enjoy indefinitely, but she supposed it was the same with photos. Put it in a nice frame, hang it on the wall and smile at it. So long as they all didn't end up online for a higher price.

Slick pawed through her goods, turning over the CDs and DVD clamshells to read the backs. Randi glimpsed his table and saw the sign perched on one corner.

Meet Sheldon Kind, TV's 'Bucky Gale'!

She'd never heard of him, or the TV show from whence he spawned.

Underneath that were positioned before and after photographs — on the left a towheaded youth with a prominent overbite and on the right the leering creeper dude now grinning at the cover of her debut album like he wanted to whip it out for a quick release.

"Man, my older brother had this poster on his wall all through high school," he said, holding up the photo of her leaning against a wall. Torn jeans tighter than her skin, crop top showing a hint of underboob and enough hairspray to fill a person's lungs and suffocate them. The photo defined barely legal. "It's no wonder he didn't have a perpetual boner."

That's it, I'm outta here. Randi set down a handful of black markers and stood. "I gotta run to the ladies'. Make sure nobody steals anything?" She darted for the nearest exit before he could answer or, worse yet, offer to walk with her.

"Oh lord," she muttered once in the safe space of the ladies' room lounge. It was a clean room with sofas and muted colored walls, paintings of calm seascapes and birds. Randi settled into a chair and let her mind go blank as people came and went. The autograph room opened for business in thirty minutes, and she decided she'd stay here the entire time if necessary — anything to avoid that jerk. Once the fans streamed in, he'd be too busy chatting up Bucky's admirers to bug her.

Assuming he had any. Or her, for that matter. Holy hell, what if people avoided their aisle the whole day?

"Randi Marsh?"

"Huh?" The last time somebody had addressed her by her real name, a nurse had been offering condolences on her mother's passing. Marsh sounded foreign to her ears now, and when the young woman in the green pantsuit held out her hand she took it and gave a look no doubt construed as befuddled.

"Have we met?"

"I'm a big fan, and hopefully more than that in the future." The woman introduced herself as Audra Genovese, casting director. Her words didn't seem to imply flirtation, and the stress on casting director gave away the reason for her introduction. Still, the woman acted with polite calm and Randi preferred Audra to TV's Bucky, so she sat back and waited for the inevitable pitch for a Z-grade movie about internet brain worms that wouldn't find a decent distributor.

Audra handed her a business card embossed with a studio logo. "My producer, Will Huxley, sent me here. I'll assume you're familiar with Harry Potter?"

"Who isn't?" Randi's mood brightened. She hadn't read any of the books, but she knew the series was poised to reach cult status. The first movie was due later in the year, but more were coming. Randi pinched the business card like a golden ticket, thinking of all the spare organs she'd hand over for even a bit part in one of the sequels.

Audra took the chair opposite hers. "I'm casting guest roles for a series slated for the fall, called *Wondermancer High*. Similar concept, set at a school for wizardry, but with a more American slant."

"I see." *Well, shit.* Like she had a shot at a big production. What Audra was proposing sounded like something that wouldn't make it to midseason. "Well, good luck with that," she said, and moved to stand.

"Randi. Ms. Marsh, please." Audra blocked her path to the door. Behind her, people paused to watch the scene but drifted toward the stalls after a few seconds. "I know it doesn't seem like a major opportunity, but the network is a hundred percent behind this show. There's already a huge promotional push and the show has a prime slot on Thursday night."

"Look, you're a nice lady, and I appreciate you thinking about me, but I was thinking of cutting back on acting. I've spent enough years mired in sci-fi schlock, but you know who might want a break?" She held up the business card as though to return it. "How about that Sheldon Kind?"

Audra's expression soured. "Ugh, no way. Everything he's done since *Here Comes Joe* has been a retread of that damn Bucky character. Plus, he's a scuzz."

Randi had to laugh at that. Audra told it straight. "I can tell you're good at your job. Seriously, though, I'm not sure about this…"

"We need somebody for a two-episode arc to start, and Will's had you in mind for the role of Aunt Rowdy all along. He'd have come himself to beg you, but the network committed him to something else," she said. "We would've forwarded you a script, but we weren't sure who was representing you now."

"At the moment, I'm a free agent." It sucked to say so out loud. After parting with Gemini she'd knocked on every door — except Derek's — looking for help. The few firms that had bothered to listen had suggested she take the reality show route. The idea of being stranded on an island or in a house or on a rocket ship to the moon with two dozen D-listers for the entertainment of others left her dejected. Right now, eight hours staring at TV's Bucky seemed less painful.

Audra nodded. "Please email the address on the card and I'll get you the details. I promise you, it's a class production all the way and an opportunity to reach a new generation of fans. Like this one."

A teenaged girl in a maxi dress, her dark auburn curls bound in a tie, wandered into the lounge and approached them. Audra, rather. The older woman put her arm around the girl and nodded. "This is one of our stars. Randi Marsh, meet Gabby Randall."

* * * *

Present Day

New York City. Same hotel as the fated television appearance, only now her room served as base of sorts while the tour hit venues in Manhattan, Jersey, Pennsylvania and Connecticut. Randi didn't rate as high a floor when she'd stayed here last, but the view of Times Square from her room was no less loud and impressive.

Following the fainting scare in Tulsa and the comeback in Lincoln, the tour had enjoyed flawless performances and appreciative crowds across the Midwest and up the Eastern Seaboard. Kristy, in particular, had gained a new following eager for more of her music, if Randi could trust the positive social media feedback. It didn't take any attention away from Randi Raucous, though. She liked and responded to as many social posts as time allowed. People still ragged her about omitting *Do It Again* from the setlist, but otherwise they rocked out with her.

Her playing improved with each show, too. The improvised solos lengthened and increased in difficulty, and on occasion a new lyric popped in her mind. She'd be snoozing on the bus or watching the crew set up the stage and she'd feel that familiar itch in her fingers and yearn for a notebook.

She fought the urge. She missed singing and performing full-time, but the pull of her work at Too True proved stronger. On the *Danse Macabre* set, people listened to her and considered her ideas. In a way, she held the position her managers had, but when she called the shots she made sure everybody working under her gave their input. She longed to be the person she'd wanted managing her younger self.

She'd see pictures of Gabby and Dash on her social feeds, goofing off with set props, and curse herself for not being there. She'd receive texts from Barry Spahn, an eager writer poised to work on *Fallen Angel*, and feel guilty she didn't have the time to mentor him.

As much as she saw this tour as a fantasy rock camp vacation, she couldn't wait to get back to California and her office in the Too True building. She wanted to sit in her chair, strum her guitar and think up strange story arcs for Steffi Corden on their new show.

What about Derek? taunted her mind as she lay on her bed, legs crossed at the ankles and hands folded on her belly. Tonight was an off night. Most of the crew had gone out earlier to try their luck at getting into a hot Broadway musical. Kristy and Zane had invited her to dinner, but she wanted to catch up on her rest. Derek…he'd kept a respectable distance this evening. It hadn't been the case during other nights, when she'd hear the deadlock give way and he'd slip into her room to 'check up' on her.

Who was she kidding? She reveled in the sex. It turned back the clock and she no longer faced middle age while in Derek's arms, under the sheets. She was Randi Raucous, rock vixen, again, and in the dark it didn't matter that Derek was thirty years older as well. He didn't feel old inside her. Her back didn't ache when she rode like him a—

She chuckled. "Am I too old to think thoughts like that?" she asked aloud. Her brain offered no answer, but her stomach cried out for attention. She rolled off the bed and pressed against the window, searching among the gargantuan neon displays for somewhere good to eat. Times Square held several fast food and gimmicky restaurants, nothing that tempted her palate. The hotel, as she recalled from her last stay, had a decent kitchen and she perused the menu when a sharp knock at the door startled her.

"Room service!" bellowed a deep voice.

"Wrong door," she called back. "I didn't order anything yet."

"Compliments of the hotel, Miz Raucous."

Right. She'd open the door to no food and a creeper in search of an autograph or a free boob grab. *No thanks.* Randi stormed to the door to tell off the interloper, but the distorted view waiting for her through the peephole caused her heart to lift with joy.

She unlatched the locks and yanked open the door to admit Gabby. "What are you doing here?" she cried. When she pulled Gabby into a hug she felt a bump and stepped back as though shocked by static. "Oh, dear, look at you." She admired the bulge of Gabby's abdomen. "Has that much time passed or are you carrying a linebacker?"

Gabby laughed and smoothed a hand down her belly. "Watch what you say. She's very susceptible to suggestion. She'll kick all night."

"Where's Daddy?"

"Getting food. I thought we'd bring it up here in hopes you haven't had dinner yet."

That suited Randi fine, and the two women set about preparing the small dining table with plates and utensils. Gabby revealed she wanted to see more than one show, and as the window of opportunity for traveling far was closing soon, they figured on a New York trip while they could still enjoy it. "I wanted to catch up with Lena, too," she added, settling down in a chair with a cold glass of caffeine-free soda. "She's been sharing raw footage of the doc. It looks awesome."

"I guess. I live it daily, so maybe somebody will find value in it." Lena wanted her and Kristy and other players to sit down afterward for interviews, clips of which would be spliced in between the concert and backstage scenes. She wasn't looking forward to that part, and decided to volunteer to be last for it.

"I had a dream the other night," Randi said. "Part of it was about Audra. You hear from her lately?"

Gabby nodded. "She still loves being retired. Nothing I say or do will coax her back to L.A."

"Well, damn. Usually when I have dreams about the past I get to thinking about whether I should have done some things differently."

"You mean like when you're back in high school and you keep skipping your worst class on purpose?" Gabby rubbed her stomach. "I hate that one. Makes me guilty for not being a better student."

"You turned out fine. One day I worry I'll dream about turning Audra's offer down," Randi said.

"Why? It's a dream. You still have a job with the company."

"I know, it's just…" Randi faded into silence. Had she said no to Audra, turned down the Aunt Rowdy role, what then? She might have continued making shitty movies or settled for appearances on celebrity editions of reality shows. The *Wondermancer High* gig, while not as regular as Gabby's, had opened better doors for her. None of them, however, involved music.

"I wonder if I could have had a legitimate shot at a comeback without *Wondermancer High* and *Danse Macabre*, you know what I mean?"

Gabby looked up from her soda and offered a grim smile. "Yeah. You wanted to get there on your own merits, without a springboard. I don't think that's what this tour is, though."

Randi gave her hard side-eye at that. "You think so? Lot of young people in the audience, wearing WH shirts."

"Young people would have come if you were never Aunt Rowdy. Parents take their kids to concerts. Ooh." Gabby made an abrupt move to stand and patted her belly. "That was a ninja kick."

"You going to be okay flying back to L.A.?" Randi asked, worried now. "I didn't think you could get on a plane this far along."

"Not supposed to," said Gabby, sipping her drink. "It's why we took the train. Don't look at me like that. We got a sleeper car."

"About to say." Randi slouched in her seat, guilt washing over her as she contemplated her next words. "I've had other dreams, too."

"Like what?"

"Playing more. Ideas for songs…" She tried to read Gabby's face, but her friend was a blank slate. The woman ought to consider a second career in competitive poker. "The tour is doing well."

"It's doing awesome, is what Lena's saying. She's had a few people talk to her about distributing a two-hour version of the docuseries for theatrical release."

Damn. This was news to her. Randi wondered what else had been kept from her. Derek had spent quite a bit of time on the phone, his voice authoritative. Wouldn't he let her in on his plans if they involved her, though? He wasn't talking to Lena, that was for sure. They shared the same bus.

"Well, y'all do what's right for the company there. If you still trust me to run *Fallen Angel* when I get back to California, I'm down for it."

Gabby set down her drink and leaned forward, arms folded on the table. "You don't sound so enthusiastic about it. I mean, I know you weren't too hip on working with Steffi Corden, or spending time away from *Danse*, but I could look at your eyes and detect some light. You look different now."

"Because I'm younger." Randi batted her lashes. "You thought I was pushing sixty for a while there."

Gabby laughed. "I meant you look like you want to grab your guitar and mess around."

"I do that at work."

"You want to do it as work now."

The mirth faded, and Randi saw a touch of melancholy in Gabby's expression for the first time. Of course, pursuing music full-time again meant leaving Too True in her friend's mind. They had a nice history, had had each other's backs for years through good and bad. Randi expected things to change. *Hell, Gabby is having a baby.* What if she decided to reduce her role at the company?

"Girl, you know our relationship won't change whatever I do," Randi said, reaching to pat Gabby's hand. "If I decide I want to return to music, you'll have plenty of notice."

"I know. I didn't mean to imply you'd up and leave." Gabby stood, wobbled a bit and took her drink to the sink. "Dash and I think of you as family. We want what makes you happy." She turned toward Randi. "I'm willing to help you work around the shows, too. There's no rule that you can't have two jobs."

"Speaking of family…" Randi understood she was about to hit a sore spot here. "Have you worked on inroads with your own?"

Her answer was a sour look from Gabby. "Dash's mom plans to come up for a while to help out," she said. "That's plenty."

"Okay." Best to leave it. The elder Randalls were known for their abrasive behavior and possessiveness of Gabby's reputation. Despite having nothing to do with Too True or *Danse Macabre*, they offered sound bites to the media that implied some involvement. It wouldn't surprise Randi to find them at the hospital when Gabby went into labor.

A knock on the door broke through her train of thought. Thinking Dash had finally arrived and needed to be relieved of food cartons, Randi offered to get the door. Her heart lifted on seeing Derek on the other side. No food, but a bottle of champagne and two glasses.

"Oh, hello!" He wasn't in on the surprise, finding Gabby's presence with wide eyes. "We'll have to get you and Dash passes—"

"No, we have our seats. We don't want any special treatment. This tour isn't about us." She winked at Randi. "Besides, Lena's hooking us up for the Hollywood Bowl."

"Is there any sparking apple juice in the honor bar?" he asked. "You could join us in our little celebration." Derek removed the foil from the bottle's neck and twisted the wire cage. What warranted all this ceremony? Tickets were selling well, and reviews were positive, but Randi had no idea about this spontaneous toast.

Derek explained as he measured out the bubbly between the two flutes. "I just got off the phone with Vivox Records, and they imparted some very good news."

"They're folding," Randi said, more from wishful thinking than an actual guess. On seeing Gabby's puzzled expressed she supplied, "Vivox is mainly a reissue label. They bought out Glissen and my other label and consequently own my masters." She shook her head, thinking of the pittance payments she'd received since the acquisition. "What business do you have with those cutthroats?" she said Derek.

"That's not the attitude to have for somebody who's been offered a three-record deal." He handed a flute to Randi, who froze in place with her hand turned up to receive it. That made no sense. Vivox bought up old catalogs and put out 'deluxe' editions of old albums and endless hits and rarities packages. One such Best of Randi Raucous CD featured an awful picture of her — blue smoky eye shadow and a horrid pink leotard the people at Gemini had sworn looked hot on her. She wanted to throttle whichever intern in Vivox's marketing department had arranged for use of that cover. Because the album featured more covers than original songs, she saw little money made from her voice and image.

"Vivox?" Am I hearing him right? "They don't put out new material."

"Not yet. They're expanding, and they want a new Randi Raucous album to launch next year." Derek clinked his glass with hers and enjoyed a healthy sip. He lowered his glass seconds later with a frown. "Why aren't you happy about this, love? This tour is an absolute success, and you're back on top...oh." He glanced at Gabby. "I hope you're not thinking I'm trying to poach your main director," he told her.

Gabby gave a slow shake of her head. "Randi will always have a place at Too True, so long as I'm running it. It's up to her if she wants to make time for albums and tours, and if she does she can have my money."

"And what Randi wants is to make her own decisions regarding her career," Randi added. She left the champagne untouched, thinking it might turn to acid in her mouth. "What gives you the right to negotiate deals for me? Especially with a label that's made money off my back?"

Derek turned defensive—his face darkened. It unnerved Randi a bit, but she refused to back down. "What if I informed you, dear, that Vivox agreed to up your residuals as part of the deal?"

"So, I'm beholden to Vivox to produce new music in order to get back payments that should have been mine in the first place. When did I ask you to speak for me at all?" Randi stood with a jerking motion and paced her suite. "I thought the whole point of this tour was one last hurrah. You get a TV show out of it, and I perform live on my own terms."

She glanced at Gabby, whose discomfort seemed to shoot up a few notches as they all exchanged looks. Gabby checked her phone—an obvious fake move if Randi ever saw one—and let out a gasp. "Oh, it looks like Dash is locked out of our room. I better go rescue him." She rose and quick-stepped to the door, all apologies and polite nods while making her escape. "We'll see ya later."

"You happy?" Randi demanded of Derek. "You scared her off."

"You're the one ranting, love," countered Derek, unruffled while sipping his champagne. "As I recall, you've been given everything you asked for. You picked your band, and we brought on Kristy despite her lack of experience. It was a gamble, but luckily it paid off."

He took the seat Gabby had vacated, nowhere close to leaving as Randi desired.

"I'm grateful you did. Sign on Kristy and Zane," she clarified. "I know we also talked about how any further work in music on my part was my decision. You're not my manager anymore. You're not authorized to make deals for me."

"It's foolish to pass it up, Randi. You don't have to leave Gabby's company, but don't you want the opportunity to sing and play your guitar again? Like you wanted that first time I saw you at the Black Alchemy show," he said, then stood to approach her. "You looked so happy, in your own world. We were all just orbiting you until you came back to Earth."

Randi thought back to that moment. Actual details had since fuzzed in her memory, but she realized she'd blocked out a lot of activity in that green room. The music had taken over, surrounding her senses so nothing else mattered. Not the jeers of so-called established rock stars, not the designs of managers who promised loyalty but made things complicated.

"Gabby trusts me," she said, and startled when Derek brushed her arm. "She knows I'm capable of directing her scripts and delivering an amazing product. I like that I can take charge in my career, and I want that in every aspect of it. That includes signing with labels."

"What do you think is going to happen if you go along with the deal I got you?" he asked. "You think they're going to tell you how to style your hair, or what clothes to wear? Songs to sing? It's a different ballgame now, love. You're not an ingenue to be molded into a corporate image. You're a legend with a profile and talent they want to raise."

"Vivox has my entire back catalog. They've put my songs in numerous compilation albums, stretching me thin," Randi countered. "I don't like how they've dangled recycling out for fans to buy."

"Give them new songs, and it'll stop."

Will it? Randi wanted to accept that, but her history with labels and management — people acting in her 'best interests' — made her gun shy. If Gabby started a record label tomorrow she'd sign in a heartbeat, because she knew Gabby would take care of her. Signing with Vivox, she presumed, amounted to a 'meet the new boss, same as the old boss' situation that unnerved her.

"I need to think about it," she said, and walked deeper into her room. She jerked her suitcase onto the bed and rummaged through the side pockets, for something to occupy her hands and mind. Her appetite gone, along with her desire to hang out with Gabby and Dash, she wanted to crawl into bed and let the night end. Let time speed up until the last date of the tour as well. This was supposed to be a fun diversion from work, not a repeat of bad history.

She felt a presence behind her and startled when Derek's hands cupped her shoulders. He pressed a kiss to the side of her head. "Randi, I'm sorry for acting on your behalf when I clearly had no right. I saw an opportunity that could benefit you, and bring you back into music, and I responded like any manager would. I suppose being on this tour, I forgot for a moment you were doing me a favor, and that this is all temporary."

"Yeah." That word had a bitter finality to it. Like summer camp. Forge amazing friendships over woven bracelets and s'mores, and once you're home you never see those people again. They'd finish the East Coast leg of the tour, then head to the Hollywood Bowl for the finale, then it would be over. She'd resume her show schedule, and Derek...

"You want I should leave you alone?" he asked. "To think?"

Randi nodded, saying nothing. Nor did Derek add anything. He released his hold on her and backed away. Randi listened for his footsteps toward the door and expected a quiet exit. Instead, his last words shook her to her bones.

"Everything I've done for you here was because I love you, Randi. Not just this tour, either."

She didn't turn around until after the door clicked shut.

Chapter Eleven

What's it gonna be?

The question sounded clear in her mind, as though the person asking it stood with her backstage. However, Greg wasn't here. He was enjoying the good, retired life in Montecito, no doubt groaning a bit from having to sit cross-legged on the living room floor to play dolls with Gwen. He'd earned his sunset, but damn it, Randi wished he'd tried to weasel his way back into her band.

She needed him, the closet thing she had to a brother and father, to appear and impart sage wisdom, not unlike a climactic scene in a film where the heroine comes to realize her true worth.

Instead she stood here, just backstage, and watched the crowd react to Kristy and Zane's set. They looked amazing together, the years melting away as the energy of the audience and the music enveloped them. Kristy's costume — a hybrid of early pop girl and neon metal chic — had seemed silly in the planning stages of the tour, but Randi saw it worked. Her friends didn't deliver an acrobatic performance, but they made up for it with her powerful voice and his heart-stopping solos.

What's it gonna be? Greg had asked her this many years ago, after breaking with Derek's firm, as they watched her opening act slog through a tinny, loud number. She'd believed then that she'd reached a nadir in her personal and professional life. The award nominations ceased, sales declined and the best she could do at the time were small venues that didn't sell out. Other, newer acts enjoyed the big-name sponsors and the lion's share of her label's marketing budget. She'd seen this screech owl of a lead singer cuss out the front row and imagined he'd soon leapfrog her up the charts.

That she still headlined at the time amazed her.

She'd wanted to quit right there. Take the stage after the opener, apologize to the crowd and leave. Greg knew it, and to this day Randi wasn't sure if he was humoring or supporting her.

'What will you do if you walk away?' he'd asked. *'You might get sued for breach for contract. It'll be hard to find another label after that bad press.'*

'I'll act,' she'd said. *'That last movie wasn't so bad.'*

'Not if you're Ed Wood.'

They'd bantered more, the words lost to time and noise. Randi couldn't recall the exact conversation but one moment stayed with her.

'Derek can put you back on top in two days. You only have to ask.'

'I think I burned that bridge.'

'For somebody who thinks she knows how everything works, you have a lot to learn.'

She'd glared at him. *'Like what?'*

Greg had towered over her, one eyebrow arched. '*Like it's okay to ask for help. You're not a failure if somebody gives you a boost.*'

'*I've told Derek no enough times, I'm sure that ship has sailed.*' Randi had also figured the drama with Gemini had turned her name to mud in the music industry. Who would touch her?

Think so? He'd tugged her elbow and pointed out into the seating area.

Derek had stood in the crowd, studying the band and scanning the corner of the stage like he might spot somebody watching.

Maybe her.

She watched as Kristy and Zane finished their final number with a flourish, then bowed to cacophonous applause and cheers. The noise surrounded Randi like a generous embrace, but she couldn't see her friends soaking up the admiration.

On the other side of the stage, standing in the wings, Derek stood. He was watching her, not them. Always on the lookout for her, at times when she didn't suspect it, she surmised.

His presumptive behavior from earlier still irked her, but she understood it now. He'd always wanted the best for her, and her happiness. Though they never discussed it, Derek had long ago seen through her fib about her age and sought to protect her as an older brother might.

From there, however, the feelings changed.

A whiff of sweat mixed with cologne and tobacco brought her back to the present and she leaned to one side when Kristy kissed her cheek. "Let Kathy top that," said her friend as the duo brushed past to the green room to relax. Randi laughed and watched the house lights come up. She had time before taking the stage, since the crew needed to put Kathy's setup together. There wasn't much to do, because the drum sets for Kathy's guy and Junior were onstage, just covered in black tarps. Men positioned equipment and made adjustments.

On the other side, Kathy's drummer came into view to study his set. With his drum tech off tonight due to an emergency, he'd been nervous to let a substitute take the job.

Derek remained in place, keeping his distance. She assumed he hoped she'd calm down about earlier. If so, he was spot on. *Guess that's why he's so good at this.* He had a knack for reading people and anticipating success. He must have seen something in Too True to arrange for recording all this madness for a streaming show.

His distance allowed her space and the time to think. She needed it.

Close to Derek, Lena paced and nodded as crew walked past. She had cameramen positioned everywhere — backstage and in the rafters for aerial shots. Randi saw her and was reminded of what waited for her back home. Security, support and steady pay. Derek may have placed a nice deal in her lap, but it couldn't guarantee her what Lena and Gabby offered.

Yet, a record deal stood to make her happy. Even with Vivox, assuming they'd play nice.

Somebody let out a sharp wolf whistle and Randi turned to see Kathy sashaying toward the stage. Her red vinyl jumpsuit gleamed and her nails were colored to match. She came up beside Randi for an air kiss.

Randi looked down at the woman's impossible spike heels. "How do you walk, or breathe?" She gestured to the tight pants.

"Carefully."

Right. Kathy executed a quick tap dance before laughing and strutting onstage. Randi just shook her head and smiled through her friend's set. Before she realized it, forty minutes had passed and the crew took to the stage once again to prepare for more music.

"Three minutes, Randi." A voice filled her ear and Randi startled. She'd had the piece on since arriving, and it felt natural to her. She should have known to expect the prompt. *Yeah. Time to get the show on the road.*

A tech handed over her guitar and made sure she was all set. Her bassist appeared at her side, ready to rock. They'd stroll out together, as they had every show previous, and tease out the opening chords to a later hit of hers they used to begin the show. Now, though, as the stage went dark and the crowd cheered at the cue, Randi got ideas.

She leaned into Gary. "You up for a last-minute change?"

He raised an eyebrow. "Only you, Randi. You'll bury us all at the end of this tour."

"It's no biggie for you. Follow my lead. Junior's sharp, like his dad, and he will know how to come in."

"Fine," Gary groused. "What's it gonna be?"

Randi told him.

"You look nervous."

Derek glanced at Lena and offered a smile. "I guess so. I upset Randi earlier, and I hope it doesn't spill out into her performance tonight."

"I heard. I talked to Gabby before the show." Lena's voice held an accusatory tone, and Derek didn't have to guess the topic of their conversation.

"Do I get the chance to explain?"

Lena shrugged. "I don't blame you for your actions. I'd love for Randi to put out another record, but knowing her, she has to want it more than anybody else." She patted his shoulder. "For the record, I wasn't thinking you were trying to steal her away from my company."

"And Gabby?"

"She has a very extensive baby wish list on her website. Get two of the most expensive thing."

It was a small price to pay for an apology, but Derek noted it.

The lights turned down and the initial notes of Randi's entrance music blasted into the night. It struck him, and made him as excited as seeing the act for the first time. Everybody else in the entourage had reached the 'been there, done that' stage of the experience, so it didn't surprise him when he saw many of their crew filtering toward the green room. Lena tapped his shoulder and invited him over for a drink. "I don't know when I'll see you again tonight, and I wanted to show you some of the footage we shot today."

"After the first song?"

She accepted that and wandered off. He hated to miss any of Randi's performance, but he loved the opening number so staying for it was non-negotiable. He'd return well before the encore and be on hand for Randi, as a friendly and supportive face.

If she wanted it.

Randi and Gary approached from the far side and the rest of her band brushed past Derek and assumed their positions. They'd wait for Randi's cue, a windmill rotation of her arm to strike the first chord of *Later*, then boom. Flashpots lighting the stage, a surge of joy through the crowd...good old-fashioned rock and roll. What Derek expected and what he heard made the difference between jubilant and damn near apoplectic.

No strains of *Later* filled the venue. Instead the twenty-five thousand or so concertgoers went wild to the opening notes of *Do It Again*.

"How y'all doin'?" Randi shouted over the extended opening. "We thought we'd try something different tonight. Hope nobody comes in late. They're going to be really disappointed."

No shit.

The band turned another round of the song's lead-in before Randi took to the microphone and let it out. By this time, a micro-crowd had gathered around him. Everybody lounging backstage must have heard the new, recognizable song. Lena, Kristy and Zane stood shoulder to shoulder with him, mouths agape until they finally broke free from the shock and sang along.

Close to the final chorus, Randi glanced in his direction and their gazes locked for a moment. The energy of her love for music surged through him, warming his blood so that his fingers and toes tingled. The corner of her mouth quirked up in a smile and she returned her attention to the crowd, dancing with her guitar toward the lip of the stage. Hands shot up before her, some snapping money shots for social media on blinking phones, others reaching out for a shake or high five, any type of connection with a beloved idol. Randi nodded along with their merriment and sang right to the front row, now a cluster of bodies jockeying for the closest spot to her.

He looked out into the sea of people. Everybody was on their feet, right to the end of the song and smooth segue into the next number, Randi's usual opener.

"Hope y'all liked that one," Randi called out during Junior's drum intro. "Haven't sung it in a long time. Nice to know I still remembered the words. Now this one I do know by heart."

The show went on. Derek shifted in place, thinking by now the group in the wings would thin and go back to business, or leisure, as usual. It seemed like more people had joined them. Concessions workers, people in charge of the medical tent.

He leaned in to Lena. "You're not getting your drink?"

"Are you kidding? Who knows what else she has up her sleeve tonight?"

The crowd must have thought the same. He swore not one person left their row for the entire set.

* * * *

At the final curt note of their encore number, Randi winced as the deafening roar of the crowd about knocked her to the ground. She leaned against Junior when the entire band came together for their uniform bow. She needed all the physical support to help her stagger offstage. Never before had a performance taken so much energy from her body. Or maybe it was a trick of the mind. She'd opened the show with her signature tune, the song she'd sworn she'd never sing live again.

The world didn't end. She didn't drop dead. She'd take this one little victory and grow it.

Backstage, people glommed onto her. She saw a fury of hands and open mouths and phones — *more friends than strangers, thank goodness* — and they blurred into a giant alien being. She had to decompress a bit before getting on the bus, and hollered at her band to lead her someplace quiet.

They found the green room and Randi settled on a sofa while Junior and Gary kept the crew and hangers-on at bay. "Give her some space," one of them said. Randi had her eyes closed and wished for a strong drink. Sounds faded, to her relief, and she moved to lie across the cushions.

"Somebody get me a beer, please?" she asked, draping an arm over her eyes. It cut the brightness that tried to stream through her eyelids, but she didn't want to fall asleep right here. She'd have to answer for the impromptu set list change, of course. No doubt Lena had a schedule for her documentary footage, and Derek...well, she knew how he felt about having decisions taken from him.

Damn, had she been right to start her set with *Do It Again*? Once word got out on social media — and she'd bet people were streaming the number on some kind of app as it happened — ticketholders for the future shows would expect to hear it too. Singing it tonight was like jumping out of an airplane. Something to do once, to say it happened.

She burrowed her face into the corner of the sofa, thinking of how to bluff the rest of the tour.

Something cold touched her leg. Her beer had arrived. "Thanks, hon," she mumbled to whichever of her buds had delivered it. "Just set it on the floor by my other hand."

"Might I join you?"

Crap. Derek. At least he sounded pleasant.

"Did I surprise you, love?"

"You're not wearing your cologne."

"I skipped it tonight. Wanted to be stealthy just in case."

She hoisted herself into a sitting position, drawing her knees up so Derek could take part of the couch. She sipped long on the cold can now in her hands before thanking Derek for serving her.

He relaxed, legs spread and one arm draped over the back of the couch. "Why not come to me about a set list change?" he asked, not demanding or angry. More curious. "You know stuff like that messes up the crew."

"I get it. They recovered well enough."

"You also should understand I would definitely have approved it."

Randi pressed her hand to her lips to stifle a belch. "I didn't realize I was changing the set list until I got onstage. Anyway, I figure if I say something beforehand and then chicken out, I'm just disappointing people."

"That makes sense." Derek nodded, and looked out at the room, where her band was picking through the sandwiches and snacks. "Give us a minute, guys?"

Her men exchanged glances and waited for Randi to give the okay before they loaded up on food and left the room. Derek's head whipped back to face her. "Randi, you have never disappointed anyone in your entire life."

"You don't know that." An unsettling feeling rippled through her gut. In truth, she'd name one person off the bat—herself.

"I mean it, love. That day I dropped you off at your house, I waited for your father to get Thai food. I needed his signature on the contract since it was obvious you were underage."

No shock at that revelation. "See there? You had to be disappointed I wasn't eighteen yet. You needed to jump through a hoop to get me signed...and why didn't just you just call my bluff in the first place?"

Derek shrugged. "Who can remember now? Maybe I wanted to humor you, see how long you'd go with the charade before you confessed. Maybe I thought if I called you out I'd scare you off. Doesn't matter now, anyway." He nudged one of her ankles and she let it go slack into his lap. "Your father talked about how proud he was of you. Everybody at Glissen predicted you'd top the charts, and Gabby and Lena think the world of you.

"Randi, love." He took her hand. The warmth of his touch shot up her arms and around her neck to her breasts, like a gentle embrace. "I was wrong to be presumptive with regards to your career. I know you don't have management right now, and I want to work for you again. Not for *Danse Macabre*, unless you want, but for your music. Even if you never tour again, there's only so much I can do. I'll get you the royalties you deserve, your music in movies and TV — "

"Yes."

He blinked, then let out a stuttering laugh. "I'm almost disappointed. I expected we'd argue a bit more before I wore you down."

"Maybe I'm tired of bickering." She leaned back, resting her head on the arm cushion. The heel of one foot brushed over his lap and the soft bulge underneath his zipper, lingering for a second in implied invitation. "Before I went on tonight I was remembering this awful gig. I got through it somehow, but at the time I just wanted to walk away. Not just from the concert hall, I mean, from music altogether."

Derek listened and massaged her foot.

"Even when we were at each other's throats," she continued, "I was happy. I got along with the band and I felt the energy. I became part of something bigger than my songs. The crowds radiated it and that just fueled me. It's why I've been tempted to cut back on the TV work. This…" She gestured to the green room, but her view extended beyond that to the stage, the people outside, the music. "This is like a drug."

"Does that make me your pusher?" Derek chuckled.

"I think manager looks better on a business card."

"Is that all I get to be?" Derek leaned closer. "I love you, Miranda Marsh."

"I love you, too." She had for a long time, even when she'd hated him, even when she'd proposed breaking it off after the tour. Derek got under her skin and remained a warm memory to pull out when she needed it. Who could say whether the infighting turned her on, or if their stars were just now aligning? *Better late than never,* she supposed.

She sat up again, scooting closer to move into his lap, and kissed him. The warmth ratcheted up several degrees, sparking a familiar desire she didn't want to cool until they moved somewhere else.

A soft rap on the door forced them apart and Derek called them to enter while she caught her breath. Junior poked in his head. "We're all heading back to the hotel. You coming?"

Soon enough.

"Right behind you." Derek waved him off.

"Junior," she called before the young man left. Junior raised a quizzical eyebrow, waiting.

"Lock that door behind you," she said, winking.

Epilogue

Six Years Later

"You doin' all right, slowpoke?"

In her heeled boots, clicking up the gravel path, Randi had several yards on her husband, who was still unfolding himself from the car. Hefting the gilt-wrapped present in both arms, she turned to watch him approach. It amazed her, his insistence on keeping his chick magnet, midlife crisis car when an SUV better suited them. She liked having space for equipment without having to rent a pull-along.

Following the Eighties Ladies concerts, Randi Raucous had embarked on one major world tour to hit spots in Asia and South America she'd missed in her prime. After that, she'd settled into a residency in Las Vegas. One weekend a month, two shows, with Kristy and Zane opening for her. They had yet to sing to an empty seat. It was a nice break to look forward to, she had the time to hang with her dear friends and it didn't interfere with her TV work. Though *Danse Macabre* had ended production last year—by Dash's and Gabby's choices and with a bang, sweeping the major awards—Randi was still riding high with *Fallen Angel*.

An SUV would be perfect for their current arrangement, but Derek liked his flash. He'd chosen the gift wrap for the party, after all. Randi had to keep her stare away, otherwise the sun's reflection on the paper blinded her.

"Why rush, love? You know they're not cutting the cake without you." Derek strolled up the walk and linked his arm in hers, pressing a kiss to her forehead as they resumed forward.

"It's not that," she groused. Well, maybe it was. Gabby and Dash had invited the entire Too True crew to this party. It was a combination birthday bash for their daughter Rowena—Randi's goddaughter—and season wrap party for *Fallen Angel*. They'd completed what Randi believed was their best work yet for the show, and she envisioned the next set of episodes would tie it all up. *Would be nice to see Steffi finally get the awards instead of just the nominations.*

"I've seen your crew eat, love. It's that," Derek said. The front door opened before Randi let go with a retort.

In her near-retirement and second trimester with baby number two, Gabby glowed in a floral muumuu, a plastic flower crown in her dark red hair. "Grab a drink, we're all in the backyard," she said after the hugs. She pointed to where Randi could set her gift with the rest, but Randi heard the rapid patter of kid shoes approaching and she waited.

Rowena Gregory was the perfect hybrid of her parents, with her mother's hair and father's movie-star smile. She bounced in from the backyard, looking like a fairy-tale princess running a 5K. Pink crinoline rasped around her with each step.

"Aunt Randi, Uncle Derek, what did you get me?" The girl collided with Derek's legs for a hug, then reached for the gift.

There was no point in stifling a laugh. The kid knew the score. Not-so-fairy godmother delivered at birthdays and Christmas.

"Rowena, we were going to wait until later," Gabby scolded, but Randi took the moment to play the godmother card and usurp her authority.

"Hey now, an old lady like me might not be around late. I want to see Rowena enjoy her present while I'm here," she said, winking at Gabby to keep her from protesting. It brought back memories of the surprise party they'd held for her on the *Danse Macabre* set. Everybody had believed she'd turned sixty, but she still had a few years to go to hit that milestone. To this day, Randi wasn't sure who all knew her true age. She had trouble remembering it herself, for all the stories she'd told. For her last few birthdays, people had played it safe and planted a single candle on her cakes.

Rowena pleaded with her mother to bend the birthday rules. Who could blame her, given the size of Randi's gift? One glance at the present table, at the collection of tiny boxes with flowing ribbons, told her Rowena held no confidence for big-ticket toy items there.

Thinking that made her second-guess her choice of gift, but the girl was grabbing at it. No time to offer money instead.

"Fine." Gabby capitulated. "At least let me get your fath—"

Nope, no such luck. Randi and Derek kneeled down with the long, rectangular box and Rowena clawed with relish at the paper to reveal a carton containing one cherry-red electric guitar.

"Yay! It's just like yours," she said to Randi.

"Almost. You see, Ro, this has Aunt Randi's name on it." Derek took out the instrument and showed the girl the gilt signature on the body. After decades in the business, Randi at last had her own line of guitars. Derek had made the deal, and Rowena now owned one of the first models.

"Randi, that's amazing!" Gabby came over for a better look. "I'm so proud of you."

"Well." She flushed, embarrassed. "Be proud of Derek. He made it happen."

"You made it happen, love," Derek said. "You're the musician. I can't do my job without you."

Their gazes locked for a moment, long enough for Randi to forget where they were. His look said he couldn't live without her, either, and the feeling was mutual.

"Will you teach me how to play it?" Rowena asked her.

"Of course. You can take lessons with Cousin Gwen." Greg and Kimberly's daughter, now in middle school, had proved a natural, though her mother preferred she stick to the violin.

Gabby took the guitar and ushered Rowena back to the party. "C'mon, kiddo, let's go show Daddy." She smiled at her friends. "Help yourself to drinks. Food will be ready soon."

"Right behind you." Randi watched mother and daughter walk away. Beyond them the glass doors revealed a backyard party in full swing. She recognized almost all the faces—most were coworkers and spouses, with a few network people scattered about. It warmed her senses and she couldn't help but smile to see a group of people she considered family. She hoped that whenever *Fallen Angel* ended, she'd stay in touch with Gabby and Dash and others here, and that whatever she took on next involved them.

Derek caressed her shoulder and drew her closer. "Where'd you go?"

"Just thinking how I'd like to freeze this moment. Live in the happy forever."

"It must have worked. You haven't aged, at least."

She nudged him. "You already got me. No need to lay it on."

"I just love you, is all." He kissed her cheek, then nodded to the party. "Come on, let's have some fun." A few steps, then, "You really going to teach Rowena guitar, too?"

"Why not? Gwen's picking it up well and there's no harm training future members of the band."

"Seriously?" He laughed.

"Seriously," she echoed. Her goddaughters had the talent and the love of music, just as she'd had at their age. All they needed was encouragement, guidance and a good manager.

Randi would give them all three.

Want to see more from this author?
Here's a taster for you to enjoy!

ExStream Love: Finish What You Started
Kathryn Lively

Excerpt

April, 2006, Las Vegas

Gabby Randall stood at the window of their fifteenth-floor suite at the Fitzgerald Hotel and Casino, looking out at the blinding lights of Fremont Street. Thousands of them, maybe a million, blinked in rapid succession, simulating waves and fireworks and starbursts in colors she hadn't realized existed. Down and to her right, a two-story tall neon cowboy winked and waved to passersby from his perch at the Pioneer Club. Bright yellow piping outlined his checkered shirt and knowing leer, and if Gabby moved one inch to one side or the other she could swear his eyes took on a sinister glow.

He stared at her, accusing her, as though to say *Shame on you, girlie. Eloping without telling nobody.* She wanted to turn away, but his eyes proved too hypnotic to resist.

"Shut up. I'm an adult," she muttered, and blinked to break the spell. The cowboy had a name. The clerk at registration had said as much, but it'd gone right out of her head, replaced by choruses of nearby jingling slot machines as Dash had given him two fake names and paid cash for the room.

She looked past the neon smirk and studied the vibrant patterns of one hotel's marquee. A thought occurred to her about the lights — how would anyone know to check for burnouts and replace the bulbs if the signs ran twenty-four-seven? Did the hotels each hire a specific person to stand on bulb duty? Were they like Christmas light strands, in that if one was faulty then the whole thing didn't light up?

Why she pondered this, of all things one wondered about Vegas, she didn't know. She took a deep breath and decided that her mind chose to focus on inane observations to calm her nerves.

It had less to do with coming to a strange city than it did with this being her first night alone with Dash. Her first night alone with any man, for that matter.

She'd never visited Las Vegas before, though she'd entertained a number of invitations from event planners. Her parents and managers, as devout in their Catholicism as their business savvy, had refused on her behalf time and again. No conventions or junkets unsanctioned by the network, or them, for her. Definitely, they didn't want her involved in a cheesy celebrity magic show or publicity stunt. Vegas might as well have been situated on the outer rim of Hell.

Now, their say mattered little. She'd turned twenty-one the previous week, on the same day her contract with Randall Talent had expired. Marie and Walter might remain family, but they no longer made decisions for her, business or otherwise. This included her most important one to date—her wedding to Dash Gregory.

Gregory. She was Gabby Gregory now. Or perhaps she should hyphenate to Randall-Gregory, and use her given name, Gabrielle. Maybe that would make her appear mature, and more professional when she met with prospective agents to help her transition from TV ingénue to a place behind the camera.

In her left hand she held the current issue of *People* Magazine, the cover of which featured her with the other five principals of *Wondermancer High*, the television show that had served as her work and home for the past six years. In her right, a marriage certificate affirming her union with Dash Gregory bent in her tightening grip. It had happened only an hour ago, and if she brought the paper closer she could smell the printer ink. Her thumb brushed the black-marker signature of the minister, a middle-aged Johnny Cash impersonator with authentic sideburns and a paunch. Dash had insisted using a fake Elvis seemed too cliché, and that his late father—a Cash fan—would have gotten a kick out of it.

Gabby had conceded easily. She'd have stood before a showgirl in all her ostrich plumage and glitter if it meant a legitimate marriage. The Cash impersonator hadn't recognized either of them, which was good. He didn't fit their show's demographic, and apparently he didn't have a teenager who forced him to sit in front of the set every Thursday evening at eight.

She set the license on the nightstand to prevent further creases, then focused on the magazine. *Good Luck, Graduates!* read the headline, in reference to the series finale due to air next month. Sadness barely touched her as she recalled the emotion and angst which had pervaded the set when they'd filmed their final scenes. Relief was more like it. She'd played the part of Tula Truebend for six seasons, and as far as the country knew, her real life mirrored that of the prim, straight-A student aspiring to the upper echelons of the magical world. Hardly. Her grades, passable enough to let her continue acting, wouldn't get her into Harvard. She hadn't planned on college, anyway.

With the series behind her now, she couldn't wait to pursue a career as a screenwriter and producer—to create rather than regurgitate. First order of business—develop a project for Dash.

Of the six main actors on the paranormal-set show—created to capitalize on the success of the Harry Potter franchise—her new husband stood to suffer the most typecasting. While she'd played the brain, a pretty one to boot, he'd been the token geek. Glasses, perpetually bent wand, goofy laugh, and no fashion sense. The showrunners had neglected all requests to mature Freddie Grodin toward the end of the run, leaving 'Grody' to remain a beloved yet awkward and inept nerd in the eyes of *Wondermancer High* fans.

She promised herself Dash would have a long acting career, and not in variations of the same role. What the hell was taking so long with him, anyway? He'd gone for water...had he tried the Hoover Dam first?

The handle of their room's door jerked and rattled, startling her. On instinct, she clutched the full-length robe she wore tighter around her chest. When they'd stood exposed on Fremont Street, walking from the chapel to the hotel, she'd fretted over possible discovery from fans and paparazzi. Instead people had brushed past them, oblivious. Only in a city like this could that happen, she realized.

"Finally," Dash muttered and entered the room. "I hate these damn keycards. They only work half the time." A plastic bag, heavy with bottles and snacks, hung from his forearm, and he wore his favorite Dodgers cap pulled low over his face. Gabby smiled upon seeing it, especially since Dash really didn't need to wear it to conceal his identity. Without the taped-up glasses and slicked-back hair the world saw on Grody each week, Dash as himself resembled nothing of the character he played. She envied his ability to roam free.

No, Dash was gorgeous with his clear blue eyes and a hint of stubble shadowing his firm jaw. He removed the cap and ruffled his short hair, adding to his adorably scruffy look.

"I'm glad you're back," she told him, and approached him for a hug. "I don't like being here by myself."

"Hey." He took the magazine from her and set it next to the license, then enveloped her in his arms. He felt safe, warm. "It's okay. Didn't I tell you we'd be all right? It's official, we're married, and there's nothing anybody can do about it."

"I keep thinking somebody saw us downstairs." Visions bloomed in her mind of photographers stalking each floor of the hotel, disguising themselves as room service. Fans pulling out their cell phones or running for the nearest pay phone to tell their friends, or worse, announce it to the world via their MySpace pages and that new site, Twitter. Guess what…we saw Tula and Grody in Vegas! Why would they be here, checking into the same hotel room? *Ooooh!*

Friends tell other friends. Somebody knows a guy at the Enquirer. He calls his contact in Vegas. Somebody calls her parents…in three seconds the SWAT team will kick down their door…

"Gabby, you're shaking."

"I just want to be a married person for one night without the world knowing about it."

Dash chuckled. It vibrated throughout her body, making her very aware of him. The robe slipped open and her breasts, hidden by a sheer layer of satin and lace, pressed against his body when he drew her against him. Her nipples hardened, anticipating his touch.

They hadn't seen this much of each other during the year they'd secretly dated. They'd kissed, a lot, and enjoyed a quick grope over clothes in between scenes. She'd saved it all for tonight.

"We're fine, Gabby," he assured her. "We could walk the whole Strip tonight and nobody is going to notice us. There's enough in Vegas to distract people. In fact," he pulled away and she whimpered, "I thought we might stay an extra night."

"But we're going to New York tomorrow." An outsider might have viewed their wedding as spontaneous, but they'd put a fair amount of planning into this week. Marry in Vegas, then off to Manhattan to shop for an apartment. Stage and TV auditions for Dash while she met with agents to discuss her ideas for projects.

"I know, but you deserve a proper honeymoon, however short. It's not like we're broke and have to go back to work immediately."

"I know." Assuming *Wondermancer High* enjoyed a long life in syndication, they wouldn't have to work again with their combined income if they budgeted well. She wanted to work, though, and intended to distance herself from Tula Truebend.

He sat on the edge of the bed and kicked off his shoes. The white Polo he'd worn for the ceremony came next, discarded onto the carpet. Dash stretched his arms to the ceiling and Gabby marveled at the definition in his muscles. She couldn't wait to trace every ridge and curve.

"I was thinking we'd go see Celine or Elton, or Cirque du Soleil," he continued, shucking his pants and socks. Clad in his boxers, he scooted back to lie on the bed. "I'll get tickets for whatever you want. I got the room for two nights either way, and New York isn't going anywhere."

He patted the vacant side of the mattress and eyed her standing form. The robe's belt had come loose, exposing her legs and the red baby-doll barely covering her thighs.

"I'm not going anywhere, either," he added.

"Good." The robe slid to the floor, and Gabby crawled up the bed and moved flush against her new groom. Dash slanted his mouth over hers, and she melted into his embrace, sinking deeper into bed as he rolled closer. She explored the smooth planes of his back on down to his cotton shorts, where she longed to discover his better assets. Limbs twined, fingers plucked at straps and elastic bands, all the while she let her husband plunder her mouth with his tongue. She tasted the coffee they'd shared earlier and a hint of mint gum, clearly used to mask the strong drink.

She'd never felt happier, being with Dash. She was ready to put Tula Truebend behind her and act her age. She'd reveled in the simple act of buying this skimpy lingerie for her wedding night, enjoying shopping like a "grown up."

Her parents had kept her under constant watch during the show's run, having everything done for her. They'd paid her bills, chosen her outfits, and watched her diet. No more. She wouldn't think about them tonight.

The straps of her baby-doll drooped down her shoulders, freeing her body. Dash broke from her lips and kissed a trail to one breast, circling the nipple with his tongue. She shivered at the sensation, as though he set her every nerve ablaze with his touch.

He looked up with glazed eyes and a swollen smile. "Did you…?"

She nodded, and her silent affirmation that she'd taken her pill sufficed. She'd gotten the prescription in secret last month, in anticipation of their marriage.

Dash returned to her breasts for a full-on assault, nipping one while kneading the other. He shifted over her, allowing her to feel the fullness of his arousal. Gabby relaxed and let him take over. His every thrust against her sex, while still in his boxers, sparked her desire, readying her to become his in every sense of the word.

No, she thought, *we'll belong to each other*. When the shorts and her lacy thong came off and he entered her with one slow, guided stroke, she bit her lip to avoid crying out and focused on Dash above her, burying his face into the crook of her neck, cooing his reassurance that he would take care of her.

"You okay?" he whispered, his warm breath roaring in her ear.

"Fantastic. Are you?"

"Yeah." He laughed, giddy like, and pushed into her again. The pain subsided the longer they lay joined, but when he reached down for her clit she cried out. She was no stranger to self-pleasure, but having Dash touch her in this way brought her to climax much quicker than she had ever accomplished alone.

"Wow." He laughed.

"Sorry about that." She'd wanted to last, but his kiss soothed her guilt.

"I love you, babe," he said, and after a second his body shuddered. He bore down on top of her, and Gabby looked down his back to see his cute ass bob faster as he filled her. The increased motion dizzied her senses, and the heat enveloping her took her breath away. She wanted to return the sentiment, tell him she loved him as much, but the words caught in her throat.

Instead, she focused on them and tried something she'd read about in a how-to manual. With him deep inside her she tightened around him and thrust. *Oh, that's nice.*

Dash reared upward, his face pinched with pleasured pain, and cried out as he released. The warmth blossomed inside her, and they kissed away their afterglow, their hands sliding across dampened skin and fisting the sheets.

I love you. The words looped in her mind, and she hoped their connection strengthened enough for him to hear it.

Dash pulled away and they touched foreheads. His lashes brushed hers and he shook with quiet laughter. "I can't wait until bedtime every night, if it's like this."

She almost made a *Wondermancer High* joke—*It's nothing like the dorms at Huntington Hall*. Instead she nodded and kissed his nose. No references to the past, she decided. They weren't Tula and Grody, who only spoke to each other when Tula needed him to get her boyfriend out of a scrape.

She was Mrs. Gregory. Now and forever.

She took the comforting realization to sleep, Dash spooning her as they turned on their sides toward the window looking out onto Fremont Street.

"What do you think?" he whispered in her ear. "Stay an extra day."

"Sure." She'd prefer to spend all their time here.

She snuggled against her husband and watched what lights were visible until she drifted away, thankful the neon cowboy couldn't see them.

* * * *

He first heard the knocking sometime around six, as the clock by him read, and bolted upright in bed when he didn't recognize anything in the room. After a few seconds his memory kicked back into gear, and he checked on Gabby. She had shifted little in sleep, remaining on her side and snoring quietly.

Still married, good. Wife here. Tired. Sleep more.

Dash waited, then settled back into bed with his arm around her, convinced one of their neighbors was being summoned from slumber. He'd arranged for room service to wheel up breakfast at eight, and he saw no reason to—

A second series of knocks, more forceful, jarred him. He cursed. Either the front desk had screwed up the delivery time or somebody had the wrong room. *Damn it.* He'd hoped for at least another hour of sleep, then waking leisurely and making love to Gabby to work up their appetite before taking on the day.

Instead he slid out of bed, found his boxers, and hopped into them as he headed for the door. "Go away," he called out. "You're two hours early."

"Open this goddamn door."

Fuck. He knew Walter Randall's hot-gravel voice anywhere. How in the hell had he tracked them here? He and Gabby had told nobody about their elopement—no co-stars, no close relatives. Definitely no meddling parents. He'd trusted only Gabby with their plans.

That meant somebody along the way had pieced it together and ratted them out. No time, though, to consider the clerk at the car rental against the woman processing their license and ceremony fee at the chapel.

"Gabby!" called out a shrill female voice. Great. Marie had come, too. Of course she had, she'd probably driven. Everybody knew the woman yanked Walter around on a leash. "We know you're in there! Open this door!"

"Huh?" The noise roused Gabby and she sat up, the sheets folded on her lap. She looked so adorable sitting there, bare-breasted with her hair sticking out in all directions. Too bad her parents had to show up and ruin what otherwise could have turned into passionate morning sex.

"Here," he whispered and tossed her robe on the bed. "Did you tell your parents we were here?"

That woke her up. "No!" She dressed hurriedly. "You never told me which hotel we were staying at, so how could I say anything even if I wanted to?"

The pounding and shouting increased into frenzied panic, and boiled Dash's blood. They were adults, for crying out loud. Never mind that they were his in-laws now, Marie and Walter Randall had no business horning in on them like this. They'd intended to break the news to family before alerting the media, yes, but they deserved at least one day to themselves.

He took a deep breath and unlatched the security chain, then opened the door. The two middle-aged talent managers — rail-thin and balding Walter in his trademark cords and elbow-patched jacket, full-figured Marie in one of her tropical explosion caftans — bustled into the space as though prepared to take down a drug cartel. Neither brandished a gun, but the umbrella

Walter wielded like a ninja might have taken out an eye if Dash hadn't backed away.

"What the hell is going on here?" Marie demanded. She paced the room with a critical eye, no doubt searching for hidden cameras. Dash knew how Gabby's parents hovered over her, shielding her from the media and men and saturated fats. It was no wonder she'd felt somewhat inhibited last night when they'd made love. She'd wanted to get married, but Dash wouldn't have been surprised to find his wife holding back at certain moments.

Turning twenty-one, and freeing herself of her parents' grasp, was supposed to change everything. Yeah, she'd legally become an adult at eighteen like anybody else, but damn, her parents and that iron-clad contract…

Marie laid eyes on her daughter and gasped in exaggerated horror. "Holy Mother…Gabby, did you have sex with him? In a cheap hotel?"

"This is not a cheap hotel," Dash protested. Not for what he paid.

Gabby belted her robe and stood up to her mother. "That's not your concern. I'm an adult and I'm not your client anymore. Even if I were still your client, my personal business is not your concern. What are you doing here?" She folded her arms.

"You're still our daughter," Walter said, also scanning the room. For what — contraband, porn, other people — Dash wasn't sure. "And we care."

"She's twenty-one years old —" Dash began, but Marie silenced him with a barking reprimand. Then she cried out again, something crumpled in her hammy fist.

"What is this? Viva Las Vegas Wedding Chapel?" Her eyes bulged as she read. "Walter, they got married!"

Walter turned toward Dash, fury reddening his normally pasty complexion.

Dash smiled. "Hi, Dad."

"Don't you 'Hi, Dad', him. You put her up to this. You tricked her," Marie accused. She stormed around the bed, wagging her finger in anger. "Gabby has a whole career ahead of her, and I'll be damned if she ruins everything by marrying too young."

Too young? They were legally adults, for crying out loud! "You mean the way you did?" Yeah, he aimed below the belt, but Dash knew Marie's history, how she'd given up a promising acting career after getting pregnant with Gabby. How she and Walter had decided instead to give their children the opportunities denied them, all for the greater good of the family.

Dash knew this, because the Randalls reminded the cast of Wondermancer High constantly. Every time Gabby had shown signs of burnout or interest in something outside of acting, they'd played the sacrifice card and guilted her back to the set. He'd admit to himself or anyone else that he fell for her partly because he wanted to protect her from her parents. However, Gabby seemed to be doing well enough on her own at the moment.

"Yes, it's my career and my life," his wife said, "and only I have a say in how I manage both. Well" — she cast a loving glance at him — "Dash and I are a team now."

Marie's eyes narrowed to slits, stabbing invisible daggers at Dash. "You're lucky we didn't call the cops on you."

"For what? We eloped. We're married. I didn't have to coerce Gabby, because she wants this as much as I do."

"That's right, Mother," Gabby added. "You can't tell me what to do. Either of you. You're not my managers anymore. In fact, I'm actively looking for new representation."

Walter snatched the marriage license, waving the fisted paper in his daughter's face. "This is not a marriage. You marry in a church, with a priest, sanctioned by God. This"—the paper tore in his fingers—"is a farce."

"Hey, don't do that." Dash reached for the license but Marie, somehow getting the umbrella without him seeing, waved the pointy end at his face.

"I should have kept a better eye on you on the set. All this time I thought Reed would make a play for her, but no…it's always the one you least expect."

His and Gabby's co-star Reed was gay and in a relationship with a screenwriter, but he let it go unsaid. He wanted to laugh at this confrontation—it had turned from frightening to ridiculous. Perhaps Marie could salvage her acting career after all, and try out for batshit crazy mother-in-law roles.

"It's a good thing we hired that private detective when we did, though we got here too late to stop the wedding," Walter muttered.

"What!" Gabby stormed to Dash's side, looking as furious as he felt. "You had us followed? What is wrong with you two?"

Her mother carried on, not listening. "It's no big deal, Walter. We can spin this. We'll call Wayne, and he'll get her an annulment…"

"You will not. She's my wife. I'm her husband. Which of these statements are you having trouble understanding?" He talked slowly now, his voice rising. Gabby had warned him that her parents wouldn't take the news well, but he didn't expect to see complete denial and scheming to undo everything while he stood there in front of them.

"Gabby, where's your bag?" Marie paced the room. "You know what, forget luggage. Get dressed. We're leaving."

Enough of this shit. Dash palmed Walter's shoulder and steered him toward the exit. "No, you know what? You're leaving. Gabby and I are on our honeymoon and don't want to be disturbed. We will call when you're ready to talk like civilized people."

"Dash, wait."

The plea in her voice chilled his blood. He recognized the tone — one of acquiescence. He'd heard it on the set often, every time Gabby'd resisted a scene in the script or a promotional obligation. Her parents would talk to her privately, and seconds later Gabby would step back in line like an obedient — and chastened — little girl.

Walter shrugged free and glared him down. He stood a foot taller than Dash, but lacked upper body strength. If Dash had to get physical to defend himself, he would.

Gabby held out her hands, playing the peacemaker. "Let me talk with them, please?" She moved closer to talk lower. "Give me a few minutes with my parents, and I'll make sure they understand they can't push us around."

Dash glanced at Walter and Marie, and walked her toward the window, out of their earshot. Vegas never shut off — the lights continued their round-the-clock sequence of blinding patterns and waves. They ought to be here alone, looking out at the spectacle, kissing and planning which casino they wanted to invade.

"I don't want you alone with them," he whispered back. "They aren't speaking rationally. They think they still control you."

Gabby looked affronted by this. "You don't trust me to handle my parents?"

"Gabby, I love you. I know what they're capable of…"

Her face turned sour, and he changed his tack, "But you're strong. I just want to be with you."

The doubt remained in his mind. He believed in his wife, but he knew Walter and Marie. Since day one of her career, they'd hovered over Gabby and counted every penny. They had other clients, but none as successful as their daughter. Her independence threatened their livelihood.

She grasped his hand and he saw her dark eyes glass over. "We will stay together, Dash. I'll talk to them, we'll straighten this out, and after they're gone we can go on with our lives. Please."

Dash sighed. He wanted to start married life off on the right foot, and keeping Gabby happy remained top priority. He kissed her cheek and stormed past Marie and Walter to where his clothes lay on the floor. He grabbed his jeans and shirt and quickly dressed, making sure he had his wallet, flip phone, and the room keycard. "I'll wait outside," he then said.

"You'll wait downstairs," Walter countered.

"No fucking way." Before Dash could protest further the older man had him by the arm.

"What?" He pushed when Dash resisted. "You don't trust us with your wife?"

A trick question. Either way he answered, Gabby might take something from it that he didn't necessarily intend. "Fine. I'll be in the lobby," he said, looking right at Gabby. "I love you. Call my cell when you're done."

Gabby nodded, biting her lip and wiping back tears. With one last look at an agitated Marie and Walter, he closed the room door behind him but lingered only a few feet away before walking slowly toward the elevator. Quite slowly.

After a few seconds Walter's face appeared as the door cracked open. "You can't fool us. We can see you through the peephole, Einstein."

"What difference does it make where I wait? I can't hear anything out here, and besides, you two aren't staying long." He folded his arms.

"Hey, we're in no hurry to go home. You want to hang out here, okay. We've got all day in this room with our daughter." Walter sneered, his canines prominent and ready to bite. Whatever, dude. If the Randalls wanted a standoff, he'd play, never mind how his bladder ached for release.

During the quiet pause of their stare down, Dash swore he heard Gabby sob in the background and made to rush forward, but her earlier plea sounded in his head. No. As much as he yearned to act the white knight, he trusted his wife. Gabby wanted to bring closure to this stage of her life and he wanted to stand by her.

That meant giving her space.

Walter's face remained lodged between the door and jamb, and Dash noticed they'd engaged the swing bar lock so he couldn't use his keycard and barge back inside if he wanted. Typical. To Dash, his father-in-law resembled the crazed Jack Torrence from the 'Here's Johnny!' scene in The Shining. He'd never unsee this.

"All right. I'm going, but I'll be back." Dash stormed to the end of the hall, checking back every few seconds. Walter surveyed his retreat all the way, saying nothing and not moving a muscle until Dash got into the elevator.

When the doors slid shut he let out a ragged sigh and reached for the button panel to get back out, but the car had started moving.

"This is a mistake." He hated that he had caved. Gabby might not see it that way, but his in-laws had no right to interrupt their honeymoon. Hearing Gabby cry made him uncomfortable. He hadn't known the Randalls to physically abuse any of their children or clients, but if they were desperate who knew what they might try, given the chance.

After an agonizingly slow descent to the ground floor, the elevator stopped moving and the doors opened to the lobby, not to the cacophony of slot machines and tourists wandering to and fro, but the collective flash of a dozen or more cameras. A head turned and a finger pointed in his direction. "There he is!" Then the scene turned into bodies, many running at him. "Dash, Dash, Dash..." Voices shouted from all directions, hands jammed microphones at his face. "Where's Gabby, and why did you take her from L.A.?"

"Did you get married, did any of your co-stars know?"

"How did you manage to keep this under wraps?"

The ambush disoriented him for a few seconds, and with the paparazzi so close, a few cameramen gathered behind him to prevent his escape back into the elevator. It worked — the doors closed before he could take a step back.

Normally, he tolerated the media, even the aggressive paps who recognized him out of his Grody guise and trailed him on his morning jogs, because what secrets can one expect to unearth while a TV actor runs through his neighborhood?

This time, though, he connected their presence with the arrival of Gabby's parents. Yeah, some photographers slept in trees to get the right shot, but he didn't doubt the Randalls had orchestrated this distraction.

He had to get back to the room, *now*.

"No comment," he said to the crowd over, and over, and squeezed through the throng, turning around to call for another elevator. The reporters refused to accept his dismissal, however, and pelted him with more questions.

He tuned them out, elbowing away microphones and lenses, pressing the up button until he chipped a fingernail. Over and over again. *Gabby*, he pleaded silently, *please be there. Don't leave me.*

"Dash, is there any truth to the rumor you've signed on to a *Wondermancer High* spinoff?" asked a slender woman in a gray pantsuit.

What was she talking about? He was done with the show and everything related to it, save for Gabby. He brushed away the mini tape recorder she held close to his face. "No comment."

The doors of the second elevator opened and the crowd surged. Several people already occupied the car, but Dash pushed forward and shouted for his floor. The man nearest the buttons, his eyes bulging at the crowd, swiped at several numbers until the doors shut.

"Thank you," he breathed out, and sagged in one corner. He was sharing the ride with a group of senior citizens, all of whom stared at him with varying degrees of curiosity and fear.

Damn it, the reporter got in, too.

"What the hell was all that out there? You in some kind of boy band?" asked a man wearing a trucker's cap emblazoned with a chewing tobacco logo.

"What about Gabby, Dash?" asked the reporter. "Do you plan to work with her in the future? Are you two in a romantic relationship? How long have you been involved with her?"

"Shut up." Dash turned away from the group, wishing he actually possessed some of the powers wielded by the fictional *Wondermancer High* students. Given the choice, he could turn himself invisible, or change this annoying young woman into a coat rack.

"Are you aware her parents have been trying to renew their management contract with her? How do they feel about you being romantically involved with their daughter?"

Well, duh. You should know the answer to that. Surely they tipped you off to us being here.

"Excuse me," piped up one of the older women. "He never said he was the girl's boyfriend. It's not right for you to assume otherwise."

Dash's gaze panned the cluster of tourists. Everybody looked at him, expecting confirmation. "No comment," he muttered.

"Did you marry Gabby Randall? Do you plan to marry her today? Do you —"

"Lady," broke in the geezer in the cap, "I think he wants you to cool it with the questions."

"Yes," agreed a second woman. A green visor sat on her silver helmet of hair. "Leave the boy alone. He's obviously exhausted by this third degree."

"Hey," the reporter snapped. "I'm doing my job here, grandma."

The golden girl didn't take kindly to the remark. "What you're doing is hounding the poor man, and you should stop. You're just like those vultures who drove Princess Diana to her death. Chasing her down that tunnel taking pictures. You so-called journalists have no class anymore."

"Oh, whose fault is that, really?" Voices rose with the car's temperature. "If people like you weren't buying up the tabloids for the news I deliver —"

"The Internet's gonna put you all out of work, just you wait."

Then the dam burst. Dash rubbed his temples as shouts of "How dare you!" and "I have every right…" volleyed between the reporter and her new detractors. By the time they arrived at his floor the old folks had her cornered, allowing him to escape.

From the distance he saw that their door was ajar, and he lost his breath. After a second he called out for Gabby and lunged headlong into the room.

Empty.

He checked the bathroom—no sign of her.

Nothing in the room remained of Gabby, except a scribbling on the hotel notepad left on the bed.

I'm sorry. Please forgive me.

He held it for the longest time, staring down at the bed where hours earlier they had consummated their marriage, now wondering if they had another chance.

Behind him, the reporter thumped into the room, catching her breath. "Dash, where's Gabby? Dash?"

~~~~~~~~~~~~~~~~~~~~~

Home of Erotic Romance

Sign up for our newsletter and find out about all our romance book releases, eBook sales and promotions, sneak peeks and FREE romance eBooks!

https://totallyentwinedgroup.us7.list-manage.com/subscribe/post

About the Author

Kathryn Lively is an award-winning writer and editor, avid Whovian, and Rush (the band) fan. She loves chocolate and British crisps and is still searching for a good US dealer of Japanese Kit Kat bars.

Kathryn is a regular contributor to the Sexy To Go authors group and enjoys the outdoors, when she's able to get out.

Kathryn loves to hear from readers. You can find her contact information, website details and author profile page at http://www.totallybound.com